MOUNTAIN MC

GRIM'S GODDESS

HALLIE BENNETT

GRIM'S GODDESS

REAPER'S WOLVES MOUNTAIN MC #3

HALLIE BENNETT

Searching for *more* mountain men? Check out the introduction to Suitor's Crossing and *heart sparks* in the *Mountain Men of Suitor's Crossing* series here[1]!

CHAPTER ONE

AMELIE

Everybody has a secret.

And mine?

A hidden life as a sexy burlesque dancer, where my inhibitions disappear and sensuality drips from every pore.

Amelie Swanson would never perform at a strip club. She's too shy, self-conscious... too good. But Velvet Venus? She's a bad girl, a dangerous woman. Confident and sultry, she thrives on teasing men.

To a point.

I don't strip to nothing, even that's too wild for my alter ego, but burlesque is all about the mystery—revealing bits and pieces of bare skin to drive the audience to distraction. The art of it has fascinated me ever since watching the movie *Burlesque* and desperately wishing to be Christina Aguilera's character.

A woman who escapes her small town for the big city and finds her dream job.

And while this isn't exactly my dream job, it's a side hustle that brings me happiness, combining my love of dance and desire to be seen.

Because men never salivate over chubby little Amelie. I'm overlooked or ignored. However, Velvet Venus never enters a room without drawing every eye to her lush curves and coy smile.

It's an intoxicating feeling.

The beginning strains of "Desperado" by Rihanna swell from the stage, and that's my cue. Sauntering into the spotlight, I exaggerate the sway of my hips and offer a little shimmy of my chest to the crowd of men gathered around the edges of the raised platform. Reveling in the freedom of the next four minutes.

As my song fades out, I take one last bow, shaking my glitter-fringed boy shorts and bra, having lost the layers of clothing I started with. Raucous applause erupts as some men shout for me to take it all off. Leaving them with a saucy wink, I ignore their pleas and skip backstage where the next woman is preparing to step out.

"You were great out there!" Luxe says, grinning in anticipation of her own set.

"Thank you! They're all yours."

The path to a communal dressing room is clogged with racks of sparkling costumes, stagehands, and more performers. It's a real production for Club Wolf's Burlesque Night, a weekly show for men and women alike.

Every other evening men can watch the regular exotic dancers strip bare, but not tonight. This is a specialty event created by Georgia, one of the co-managers of the club. She runs it with a member of the Reaper's Wolves MC—the motorcycle club that owns Club Wolf.

Which means my hidden hobby sits precariously close to being discovered now that friends of mine are loved-up with Reaper's Wolves members. But I couldn't resist the temptation of trying burlesque when they first announced the weekly event.

There is freedom in having this one thing for myself.

Not that I don't trust my friends or believe they'll support me because they one-hundred percent will. But keeping my secret means there's no pressure to act a certain way—to be Amelie versus Venus.

They're two sides of the same person but only one gets to see the light of day.

Maybe someday I'll feel comfortable enough to reveal this naughtier side of myself. Preferably with a hot man who adores me no matter what. But until then, I'll disappear to Club Wolf every Tuesday night and dance to my heart's content with no one the wiser.

Not my family.

Not my friends.

No one.

CHAPTER TWO

GRIM

A high-pitched scream pierces the air as Goldie wobbles on stage with a broken heel, desperately clawing at the stripper pole to no avail. Without the stability of the pole, she falls backward into the crowd of men drinking at a table to her right.

Fuck.

Motioning to Ranger, one of Club Wolf's bouncers and a member of the Reaper's Wolves MC, we both converge on the spot where Goldie lies prone on the laps of two men, their hands seizing the opportunity to grab at the poor woman's exposed flesh.

"Hands off, assholes!" I bark before helping Goldie to her feet. Immediately, she groans as her leg gives out beneath her.

"Shit, I think I sprained something," Goldie whines. "These were brand new shoes, too! Two hundred bucks just to break on their first night out?"

I would never spend that much on a pair of shoes, especially not the glittering death traps currently hanging from Goldie's feet, but what do I know about women's fashion? Spindly heels that easily snap and harm their owner seem less fashionable and more ridiculous to me.

"Let's get you backstage. We'll call Saber to check things out. Until he signs off, you're on medical leave," I say. Ranger scoops her into his arms and heads to the dressing room behind the large stage while I signal for the next girl to start her routine.

Starr nods and slinks across the floor before making a flying leap and catching the silver pole at center stage. The audience quickly forgets Goldie and starts whistling for our newest dancer instead.

I run a hand through my short hair and sigh. We just hired Starr to replace a dancer who left, and I don't want to go through the interview process again if Goldie has to be out for longer than a few days. We're just now settling back into a good routine.

Club Wolf is a popular gentlemen's club in the heart of downtown Everton, the classy counterpart to the MC's second club on the outskirts of the city. While Diamond caters to truckers needing a break from the highway, and the regular Joe searching for a sexy pastime after work, Club Wolf provides an upscale experience for local businessmen looking to lock down deals over drinks. Loosening up potential partners with the allure of bare tits and juicy asses decorated in shimmering thongs.

"How's Goldie?" Georgia asks from her position behind the bar. My sister co-manages the club with me since she's the one with an actual business degree.

The brains to my brawn.

I was pissed when she went over my head and asked the Reaper's Wolves MC president if she could run the place after getting her master's. I didn't exactly want my baby sister hanging around the douchebag Wall Street types we get at the club, but Snow liked the idea of family working together since that's the whole idea behind the MC in the first place.

A home for drifter military veterans.

A found family for guys desperate for connection.

To be fair, Georgia is a godsend, dealing with a ton of admin crap behind a desk, which allows my role to be more hands-on. With my time also split between the two clubs, it helps that her focus is solely on Club Wolf, while someone else fills the co-manager position at Diamond.

"We're hoping it's just a sprain."

"At least she'll be able to rest tomorrow, no matter what." A satisfied smirk follows the statement as my sister leans across the bar to set a bottle of water in front of me, knowing I never drink on the job.

Rolling my eyes at her smug attitude, I put my back to the bar counter and scan the crowd of customers, ready to step in if anyone decides to get too chummy with the dancers. "I get it, Georgie. Burlesque Night is a hit, and it's all thanks to that big brain of yours."

She suggested the themed evening two months ago, presenting evidence to support her theory that burlesque is an underutilized goldmine. Classy. Sensual. A perfect fit for our brand and an opportunity to expand our reach to the women's market.

Because women don't care for naked girls just for nudity's sake. But burlesque is a whole other ballgame. It offers a story. Teases the mind, not just a man's dick. At least that's what Georgia said.

Seemed she was right.

"I'm waiting for a *Thank you, Georgie, for increasing profits. You're a genius, Georgie, I'll never doubt you again.*"

"Let's not go too far." I laugh. "Am I still taking Biscuit to the vet when I go with Tiny tomorrow?"

"Smooth. Avoidance," she says but nods. "Yeah, thanks. I forgot about his check-up when I scheduled the meeting with another local brewer."

"Cool. I'll pick him up around noon. Tiny's appointment is at 12:30." Tapping the bar, I tip my head in farewell before patrolling the perimeter of the club.

There's only so much of my little sister's bragging I can take when I haven't even attended a Burlesque Night to properly judge it. That'll change tomorrow.

Hopefully, I'll see what's so popular about women choosing to *not* bare it all.

Because I sure as hell don't get it.

CHAPTER THREE

AMELIE

Why do I feel so scared? Like I'm about to cry or throw up all at the same time?

Tears prick behind my eyelids as I take another careful bite of my breakfast muffin. Waking up at 5 a.m. certainly didn't help. Especially when I fell asleep after midnight.

But anxiety attacks couldn't care less when they happen.

Or how inconvenient they can be.

My jaw slowly works to chew the banana nut pastry, crunching on walnuts, rolling the tiny bite around in my mouth, before swallowing and sipping my water. Because I don't want to compound my problems by drinking coffee, no matter how much I crave it.

Another bite of the muffin.

Slightly salty. A little grainy. *Mindfulness.*

It needs to start working its supposed magic as I focus on the taste and texture of my breakfast rather than my racing heart and freezing extremities.

"Can you turn that off?" Jenna, my coworker in the next cubicle, peeks around the gray wall separating us and points to the space heater between my feet. "It's stifling in here."

"Sure, sorry." The constant heat instantly disappears once I twist the knob, and immediately, my toes go cold again.

Another symptom of today's anxiety—icy chills during the summer. Requiring the strength of my space heater to keep me warm until someone, usually Jenna, complains.

While there isn't always a concrete reason, the rush of anxiety pummeling my body currently is most likely caused by Mabel's vet appointment. I found a scabbed-over bump on her backside last night. The internet said it could be all sorts of things ranging from benign to life-threatening, so I immediately scheduled a lunchtime appointment with my cousin Winston, who also happens to be a veterinarian.

"I don't know how you're not sweating through your cardigan. It's not that cold." Jenna always adds one last snide comment before retreating to her cubicle, and I blink back another wave of tears.

I'm not the only one who brings a jacket or blanket to combat the icebox temperature of the company's air conditioning, but I am the only one who also needs a space heater. And Jenna loves to complain about it.

I hate drawing attention to my issues.

It's not that I like creating a sauna in our area, and I'm not so inconsiderate that I don't understand where she's coming from, but half the time, Jenna isn't even at her desk to feel the heat. She's busy gossiping with Kelly two rows over, and their voices carry with every bitchy comment.

Like a few hours later when the alarm goes off for my lunch break. Now, they're gossiping about Megan, who's come in late twice this week.

Shrugging off the fleece blanket draped over my lap, I fold it over the back of my chair before grabbing my purse and heading out. Thankful for a reprieve, despite the summer humidity slapping me in the face as I walk across the parking lot.

"Great, now I'll go from icy toes to sweaty pits." My body loves to swing like a freaking pendulum between the extremes, though it's been regulating itself a little better since my meds got adjusted a month ago.

Everything was going well until my doctor got concerned over my blood pressure, and thus began an arduous few months of messing with medication types and doses until I ended up back where I started. On the same meds that worked, but now I have to track my blood pressure to ensure it doesn't get worse.

Let's not add another concern to the mountain of worries today, okay? You're already hanging on by a thread.

I sit in my car for a couple of minutes to regulate my breathing. *One thing at a time*, I remind myself, then start the engine.

The busy lobby of Winston's veterinary practice greets me with a chorus of woofs and meows after I run home to pick up Mabel. The office is located in Suitor's Crossing which is a forty-five-minute drive from where I work, but it's worth the trip to see my cousin and a vet I trust.

"Hey, Linda. Mabel's here for her appointment."

The older receptionist smiles and waves me to a seat as she continues talking into the phone. She knows who I am, so there's no paperwork to fill out.

I readjust my grip on Mabel's carrier and turn to find every seat taken except for one, a spot next to an enormous man and his pit bull.

Oh, crap.

He looks familiar.

Like Reaper's Wolves MC familiar.

Ever since one of my best friends married the club's president, I've been to the MC compound multiple times and met a couple of its residents. Big, hulking men with military experience and a love for leather. Hot and unattainable—at least in my mind.

I've seen this one from afar with his dog. They like to stroll along the edges where the forest meets mowed grass. Unfortunately, his name escapes me. When we were hanging out on the clubhouse porch, Caroline told me once, but I didn't commit it to memory, knowing I'd never remember all the guys' names.

Doesn't matter. You don't have to talk to him. It's not like he knows who you are.

The realization knocks some sense into me as my legs carry me across the waiting room to the seat on his right. His dog sniffs at the carrier where Mabel whines, but otherwise, he seems uninterested.

Just like his owner.

Lots of pretty women spend time at the clubhouse—certified biker bunnies—and Caroline even told me how Snow kicked one out after she refused to understand he was taken. So this guy has plenty of options at home to pique his romantic interest.

It's certainly not going to be me.

Although my alter ego might have a chance.

But you're keeping Velvet Venus a secret, remember?

I fidget in the seat, squeezing closer to the chair arm, but whether these seats are extra small or my neighbor's extra large, the situation becomes awkward when my wide hips press against his side. We're in one of those double chairs with two cushions but no middle divider to keep us separate, and I can see why no one else chose to sit here.

"Sorry," I mumble, readjusting to find a better position, one where I'm not smashed against a rugged biker whose heat is sparking all sorts of explosions in my poor anxiety-ridden body.

Calm down before you worry yourself into a panic attack!

"You're good. I'm the problem here, not you. My body isn't made for standard run-of-the-mill shit. That's why I own a giant ass truck and a king-sized bed."

Images of his bed flood my imagination, and I fight to keep my features neutral rather than shocked at the personal details.

He shifts so his torso twists to face me, allowing a sliver of space between our arms, though his hard thigh remains pressed into mine. "I'm Grim," he gestures toward his dog, "and this is Tiny."

"Amelie and Mabel." I pat the pet carrier in my lap where my cat continues to mewl. She hates being confined to her carrier, no matter how many mesh windows it has to let her see out. "What made you name this guy Tiny? Was he the runt of the litter or something?"

I offer my palm up for Tiny to sniff, and after a brief moment of his wet nose pushed into my hand, he gives me a friendly lick, his stubby tail wagging furiously.

"Nah... When I adopted him, he was already built like a behemoth. Weren't you, bud?" Grim scratches behind the pit bull's ears, and my heart melts at the sight, my insides going all gooey.

It's like when women see men with babies. How the guys showcase a gentleness hidden behind an exterior that could easily harm the little bundle. How they choose to use their strength for good. For protection.

Geez, this isn't a Hallmark movie!

Clearly, my heart isn't the only thing that has melted. My mind's gone to goo, too, if I'm doling out chivalrous traits based on a man petting his dog.

"It's kind of an MC tradition where your club name is opposite of your personality or whatever. So, this guy's built like a tank? Gotta name him Tiny." He shrugs as if it makes perfect sense.

Following his logic, I ask, "Does that mean you're always happy? If your club name is Grim?"

A bellow of laughter erupts from his barreled chest, drawing the attention of the people around us. "Hardly. The Reaper's Wolves don't always walk in line with typical MC rules. They call me Grim because I like to play devil's advocate and voice worst-case scenarios."

"Sounds like my brain ninety percent of the time," I mumble.

"I'm sorry to hear that. It must suck not being able to turn it on and off."

"You have no idea." Just then, Winston comes out to the lobby and calls for Mabel. "That's us. It was nice to meet you."

"You, too, Amelie." The way he says my name has me itching to shove my cat into my cousin's arms and return to Grim, eager to hear him say it again. Which is totally out of character for me. I don't scramble back to men just because they make my name sound like the sexiest thing on the planet.

I don't scramble back to men at all.

Because they overlook me.

They don't see me.

But Grim did.

Hard not to when you were wedged against him like a missing puzzle piece.

The cynical part of my mind tries to bring me back to my senses, but the dreamer in me shuts her up with a quick slamming of the metaphorical door. Where's the harm in feeling excited by a conversation with an attractive man? It doesn't need to lead to anything to give me a bit of joy.

It's a nice distraction from the anxiety that's been plaguing me since last night, so I'll take the win, however small.

Won't my therapist be proud?

CHAPTER FOUR

GRIM

The bass vibrates through the walls as I stare down at the stage from the vantage point of the VIP section. The club has two levels, but the second level is only available to special patrons—those clients willing to pay a premium for privacy.

It's Burlesque Night, and my first opportunity to see what all the excitement is about.

Snow has been keeping me busy in Suitor's Crossing helping Timber and Alaska get the MC's new gym renovated and ready for business, so I've been stretched thin between that and the two clubs. But now that Alaska has things in hand with the gym, I can finally focus on Club Wolf's latest attraction.

So far, a mermaid, nurse, and bride have performed routines. All sexy. All stopping just shy of revealing everything to the crowd. A crowd that's more balanced between men and women than I've ever seen.

My pocket buzzes, and I pull my phone out to find a message from my sister. The next to last performer of the night is about to take the stage and Georgia wants to make sure I don't miss her. Someone called Velvet Venus.

A slow jazzy number comes through the speakers and I direct my attention back to the stage where a single spotlight lands on a woman dressed as a 1940s candy striper.

"Holy fuck," I whisper, placing my hand on the balcony railing for balance since the wind feels knocked out of my lungs. The outfit isn't overtly sexy. It's buttoned and zipped together in a perfectly respectable manner, but it hugs generous breasts and hips, smoothing over the woman's curves as she slinks forward.

Lyrics start to filter through the haze fogging my brain.

"*Come here, big boy.*"

My throat is dry. My tongue stuck to the roof of my mouth. I don't want to miss a minute of this goddess's performance, but I hate having this barrier between us. Making a split decision, I hurry downstairs until I reach the ground floor, eating up the space between us with my booted feet until I'm a mere yard from the stage.

The woman looks vaguely familiar, but it's hard to discern her features under the shifting lights. Her entire routine plays with shadows as much as her clothing.

In my absence, she's lost her gloves, her bare fingertips trailing over the pocket on her left breast and drawing a line over her round stomach to end provocatively over her pussy. *Damn*. This is what I've been missing all these weeks?

With each lyric, she teases with a wiggle of her hips and bold winks until our gazes clash and lock, a spotlight brightening her pretty face. Recognition zaps my body to attention.

It's Amelie from the vet office.

Amelie is Velvet Venus? And she's been dancing here for weeks?

She breaks eye contact to continue her performance, but every once in a while, I catch her glancing my way. Her moves aren't as fluid as they were before she caught sight of me, but they're still sexy as hell.

Eyes on me, sweetheart, I silently command each time her gaze skitters away.

Though I pretended not to know who she was at the vet office, I knew Amelie was a friend of Caroline, the club president's wife. I've been present enough times during the women's book club to remember that shy smile and round curves, even if we'd never officially spoken before yesterday.

Amelie's act is coming to an end as she shimmies off the striped uniform to reveal a silky scrap of lingerie. The little triangles forming the bodice barely contain her breasts. They're overflowing the sides, jiggling with every movement, and I know I'm not the only man waiting for a pink nipple to pop out.

An unbidden growl rumbles from my throat as I glare at the men filling the tables surrounding the stage. I didn't give a fuck about the dancers before and all the men who watched them, but Amelie is different. I don't want anyone salivating over her beautiful curves except for me.

She escapes offstage with a backward glance in my direction, and I take that as my cue to follow her. I'm going to have a discussion with the little goddess, and she's going to tell me what the hell she thinks she's doing.

Because I don't think her friends know about her secret, otherwise Caroline and the rest of her book club would be here cheering on their friend.

No, I think little Amelie has a hidden naughty side, and I'm just the man to explore it. She's practically begging me to by showing up in my club dressed to kill and dancing like a damn siren.

I weave through tables until I reach the door to a hall that houses the dressing room for the ladies. There isn't much privacy back here, but with only one dancer left, most of the other girls have cleared out.

Make-up litters the vanity countertops, and glittering costumes hang haphazardly on a rolling rack against the wall. But no Amelie. She couldn't have escaped that fast.

"Hey, there you are." Georgia hurries into the room with a huge smile on her face. "What'd you think? It was awesome, right?"

"Yeah," I say distractedly, my gaze bouncing around, searching for where Amelie could have gone. "Did you see where Amelie went?"

"What?"

"Amelie, Velvet Venus, the act you wanted me to watch."

"I know who she is. I'm just surprised you know her real name."

"She's friends with Caroline." And that's all my sister is going to get. I'm not explaining how we ran into each other at the vet or that I'm determined to be the only man she dances for in the future. Because that last part sounds crazy even to my ears, so I know Georgia will have something to say about it.

"Oh, she usually books it out of here pretty fast once her set is done. She's probably in the parking lot."

"Damn it." I rush past Georgia to the exit at the end of the hall and throw open the heavy door.

Bingo.

Amelie is struggling to balance on one foot as she adjusts her shoe. She hightailed it out of the club so fast she wasn't even fully dressed, no doubt in an effort to avoid me.

I don't know if it's because of her natural reservedness, or if she's worried I'll spill her secret to Snow, who will tell his wife Caroline. Either way, I'm glad she miscalculated.

Because her hurrying and making mistakes, like not putting on her shoes right the first time, is to my advantage, as I stalk up behind her.

"Leaving so soon?"

CHAPTER FIVE

AMELIE

Oh, shit. My eyes closed in defeat. After catching Grim's eye during my dance, I figured I could outrun him and avoid answering any awkward questions.

I don't know why I thought he would follow me in the first place. Whether it was something in his tense demeanor or the blaze ignited in his green eyes. But I had a feeling he'd come after me.

Maybe to warn me off the stage.

Maybe to ravish me behind the stage curtains.

Keep dreaming, girl!

Inhaling a deep breath, I turn around to face him, angling my head back to view his much larger frame. "Hey."

"Hey? That's all you got? How about an explanation for what you're doing here?" He crosses his arms over his massive chest, causing the muscles to bulge beneath his sleeves.

Why does he have to be so attractive? He's not handsome in the traditional sense. Too rough and stocky. But he ticks all of my boxes. And that's a problem.

Why is it a problem?

This is usually where I'd spout something about a guy like him never going for a girl like me. But a guy like him *did* go for a girl like me. The Reaper's Wolves MC president and my best friend Caroline. But just because it worked for them, doesn't mean it would work for us.

"I like to dance. Is there a problem?" I ask, sounding braver than I feel. Must be residual Velvet Venus confidence.

"Yeah, there is. Because a girl like you shouldn't be flaunting yourself for just anybody. Especially the assholes in there."

"And who should I be flaunting them for?"

"Me." He steps forward suddenly, his arms uncrossing to land on either side of my body, caging me against the wall of the club.

"Y... you?" I stutter. This has taken a turn. A hot and potentially sexy turn. What would all the heroines in those romance books I read do? No, what would Velvet Venus do with the prospect of a growly biker desiring her?

It's at this time my mind decides to draw a blank.

And this is why you're single.

"I wanted to ask you out at the vet's. But you seemed so chummy with Dr. Winston, I second-guessed myself. I won't be making that mistake again."

My nose crinkles in confusion and a little bit of disgust. "Winston is my cousin."

The admission surprises Grim. *Or pleases him*, I suppose, based on the smirk forming on his mouth. White teeth gleam behind the growth of his beard.

"Cousin. Well, thank fuck for that."

The words barely register before the press of his firm lips against mine has me grasping for purchase. Seeking something to ground me. I find Grim's broad shoulders, my fingers digging into the muscles as he steps closer so my entire body is trapped between cool concrete and hot man.

Two things immediately become clear.

Lust feels scarily close to anxiety with the rapid pounding of my heart and the tingling sensation traveling down to the tips of my fingers and toes.

And Grim is packing some serious heat in his jeans because the thick ridge of his erection pressed against my core rivals my favorite dildo.

"Open up, candy girl. I want to sample your sweetness for myself," he demands with a light bite to my bottom lip. A stray thought about what I ate last slithers to the forefront before disappearing with the rasp of Grim's tongue on mine.

Kissing to combat anxiety.

Did I just cure myself?

A slightly hysterical laugh gets buried between us as I throw myself wholeheartedly into Grim's embrace. The endorphins are working fast, and I feel kind of loopy with excitement. My guard walls don't usually lower so quickly.

"Don't stop," I beg when he pulls away, but it's only for a breath before his mouth devours mine again. Our groans of pleasure fill the air as we continue to make out against the club building.

This feels dangerous.

Bad... in the most delicious of ways.

Good girls don't let men maul them outside strip clubs. Let a man's rough palms cup their breasts where anyone could see. Let a man's hard arousal drive between their thighs like feral animals rutting in the wild—in public.

But that's what Grim's doing to me. What I'm craving from him alone.

Hmm... Maybe I knew what Velvet Venus would do all along.

CHAPTER SIX

GRIM

A chorus of booing hits me the moment I step into Club Wolf the next evening. *Who the hell boos at a strip club?* There are naked tits and ass, just what the pricks came for.

"What's going on?" I slide behind the bar, where a frazzled Georgia is frantically pouring shots of tequila.

"Oh, thank god, you're here." Relief suffuses my sister's features as she shoves a tray of drinks into my hands. "We're short-staffed tonight due to some freak illness that's taken out half the waitresses. And as if that isn't enough, something is wrong with the dancers' costumes. Luxe's booty shorts wouldn't unzip, and it looks like Cinnamon's top refuses to rip open like it should."

She nods toward the stage where Cinnamon keeps tugging on the sides of her sequined tank. "The guys are getting pissed. They came here to have big boobs thrust in their faces, not to witness wardrobe malfunctions."

"Not sure what you want me to do about it. I don't know anything about women's clothes. That's your department."

Georgia rolls her eyes before staring at me like I'm an idiot. "Yeah, but I can't exactly leave the bar. Alcohol is the only thing keeping people happy. I need you to handle drinks while

I check out what's going on in the dressing room before we have a riot on our hands."

Men in suits crowd the bar while the two waitresses who avoided getting sick scramble between packed tables of guys shouting their displeasure. It doesn't look like a riot is that far off. Customers are definitely unhappy.

Sighing, I send off a quick text to Timber asking him to rally some backup for the club. "The cavalry should arrive soon. You head backstage and make sure the next shift of girls' outfits works properly. Then switch everyone out. Cinnamon and Candy can come on later once they figure out the costume shit. I'll tend the bar, and if anyone has a problem with it, Grizzly or Steel will haul their asses out of here."

At least whatever plague hit the wait staff skipped over the MC members serving as club security tonight. And, hopefully, last night's dancers.

The thought of Amelie in pain doesn't sit well, and I curse myself for not getting her number after our kiss. But could I really be blamed for the mistake? She burst into my life—after months of sticking to the edges with her friends—then gave me the sweetest, hottest kiss I've ever had.

We made out until both of our mouths were bruised and patrons began filtering out of the club after the last call. Of course, any brain cells I had left were fried.

Lucky you manage the club where she moonlights every Tuesday evening.

A fact that has poked at me all fucking day. Conjuring crazy thoughts like stealing her number off her personnel file, except that feels predatory as hell. Because, technically, I'm her boss, even if it's only for the hour she spends here during Burlesque Nights.

But she could be sick. Home alone with no one to care for her.

An image of Amelie shivering in bed with a fever and then puking her guts out with no one to hold her long curls back amps up the tension in my shoulders as I work on autopilot behind the bar.

Worry gnaws at my gut, forming a black hole of unacceptable possibilities. *Fuck it.* I want to check on Amelie, and if she's fine, I'll apologize for the misconduct and ask for her number the proper way. No harm, no foul.

As soon as Timber arrives with two newly patched members of the club, I drop my final round of beers on the bartop, intent on escaping to my office to check the employee records.

"Where are you going? It's still all hands on deck," Georgia says, catching me by the arm on her way back to the bar.

"Club business."

She scoffs and raises her brow as she casts an exaggerated glance around the building. "This *is* club business."

"You, Timber, and the guys can handle it. Sorry, sis, but this is more important." I extricate myself from her grasp before she launches into a lecture on responsibility.

Something I don't need to hear.

I'm well-versed in duty and honor, thanks to the United States military. It just so happens that Amelie now finds herself at the top of my list of priorities.

CHAPTER SEVEN

AMELIE

"**A**lright, spill it," Kat orders as she plops down onto the leather couch. Caroline is hosting our book club tonight, so all of us are scattered around the open living area of the Reaper's Wolves clubhouse versus her smaller cabin.

We've grown since we originally started, adding Lindy and Faith to our ranks, and it makes me happy how this idea for a romance book club blossomed into a safe space to chat with friends all while enjoying smutty goodness. Both Lindy and Faith have been through tough experiences—what with a physically abusive ex-boyfriend and an emotionally abusive father—and I admire their strength and bravery.

Because it's more than I have.

They've dealt with trauma that would leave anyone hesitant to share, yet they opened up to our entire book club, offering vulnerability rather than silence. And here I am still living my secret double life as a burlesque performer.

"Spill what?" The gulp of sangria in my mouth tastes sickly sweet. Does she know about Velvet Venus? Or about the kiss with Grim? I don't know which would be better—being scolded for keeping my dancing persona a secret or grilled about a relationship development with Grim.

Not that we're in a relationship.

We've had one conversation in a crowded veterinarian office and one passionate kiss in a club parking lot. He didn't even ask for my number afterward, and I was too dazed to remember to offer it.

"What's got you wound so tight," Kat elaborates, flicking her hand through the air. "You came in with a pinched expression as if one of the MC guys were going to pounce at any second. No offense!" She calls behind us to the four men sitting around a poker table with cards in hand. It's clear they weren't listening, though, because we get identical stares of confusion before they return to their game.

"You were imagining things. Nothing is wrong." I did enter the compound with more trepidation than usual, nervous about running into Grim, but I'm not ready to share those details yet.

First dancing, now Grim. Since when did I become someone who hides things from her friends? My first secret has snowballed into two, and the weight of them feels heavy on my chest. The longer I wait to tell them, the harder it's going to be. The more my mind builds it into a terrible confrontation and betrayal, even if logically I realize that's not true.

Sure, the girls won't be happy about me withholding key information about my life lately, but they're not the type to ditch a friend over mistakes. My head and heart—one ruled by sound reason while the other is fueled by anxiety—are having trouble syncing, though.

"Mhmm..."

"Amelie knows if anything changes that we're here for her," Caroline interjects, ever the mediator. She adjusts her glasses—the reason for her husband's pet name for her, Little

Owl—and prompts Beth to start explaining the craft we're doing tonight instead of discussing a chapter.

We like to mix things up during our meetings, and since one of Beth's resolutions for the new year is to actually use the craft supplies she constantly buys, it was suggested that we make a bookish craft. A silly scrapbook page dedicated to our favorite book boyfriend.

"This reminds me of my middle school crush on Danny Blum." Lindy swipes a glue stick across her pink and yellow cardstock and sticks a cut-out picture of Theo James in the corner. "I drew a heart around his picture in the yearbook and added little butterfly stickers between our photos. He was two rows below me."

"For me, it was Jensen Cole." An image of the blonde-haired blue-eyed boy pops into my head. Our teacher paired us together for a science project, and rather than laze around in class, he participated, pulling his weight on our homework unlike some of the other boys.

"Adam—" Caroline's answer is cut off by her phone buzzing incessantly. "Sorry, it's Logan." Or *Snow* as everyone else calls him. Her husband. She types out a quick response, her forehead wrinkling as she shoots a glance my way.

"Is everything alright?"

"Yeah, he just wanted to know if you were with me."

Everyone's heads swivel to stare curiously at me, but it's not like I have a clue why an MC president would care where I am. "Did he say why?"

"Amelie Rose! What the fuck is the point of having a cell phone if you're not going to answer any of your damn messages?" The booming voice boomerangs around the large room as Grim slams the front door open and stalks inside. Anger radiates from his pores as he stomps toward me with long strides of his booted feet.

How does he know my middle name?

Flipping my phone over, where it's been forgotten on a side table, a blast of notifications flashes across the screen. Each one showed an unknown number and messages that increased in urgency.

UNKNOWN: *Hey, it's Grim. A bug is going around the club. Are you okay?*

UNKNOWN: *Amelie, are you sick?*

UNKNOWN: *Where are you? I'm coming over.*

UNKNOWN: *Answer your messages, baby. I'm getting worried.*

UNKNOWN: *Amelie!*

My friends know how terrible I am at responding to texts. I leave my phone on silent because the vibrating and ringing annoys me, but Grim doesn't look like he'll accept that as a reasonable excuse for ignoring his barrage of messages.

"Yeah, Amelie Rose, what's the fucking point?" Kat leans forward with a gleam in her eyes as she stresses my name in a mocking tone. Damn, I'm never going to hear the end of this now.

Hustling to my feet, I meet Grim halfway across the living room, hoping to divert him to somewhere more private for whatever showdown this is going to be. I don't know why he's so worked up over a couple of missed texts. It's not like a rogue virus sweeping the Club Wolf employees would've killed me.

"Can you lower your voice, please? You're causing a scene." My eyes darted to the guys who stopped their card game to watch us with varying degrees of interest.

"Maybe if you'd answer your phone, I wouldn't be so pissed. For all I knew, you could've passed out at home, hit your head on the way down, and been lying in a pool of your own blood."

"Wow... You weren't kidding about the worst-case scenario thinking," I say absently. His escalating thoughts of doom rivaled mine.

"Don't be cute. I almost drove to Everton to check on you before thinking to see if Snow knew where you were." Ragged breaths pumped through his chest and his nostrils flared. No one's ever been this worked up over me—little ole Amelie.

A warm feeling melts into my bones as I try not to smile. Grim doesn't seem like he'd take my flattered amusement very well.

"Why were you so freaked out?" Kat asks from the sofa.

Grim doesn't break our eye contact. "Some kind of flu is going around at the club. I thought Amelie might have caught it, too."

Panic wipes out any calm I might have felt before because he essentially just outed me to my friends. *Shit.* Their reactions shouldn't make me nervous. They're supportive and kind, and I know they'll cheer me on, but this was my secret to share. It was my private oasis from my regular life. Now it's demolished.

"How would you have caught something at the club?" This time the question comes from Caroline. Sighing in resignation, I turn away from Grim to face my friends—all of them struggling to put the puzzle pieces together.

"Because I'm a dancer at their Tuesday night burlesque event," I admit.

"No fucking way."

"Holy shit!"

"Why didn't you tell us?"

A round of questions erupts from the group, and I glare at Grim. This is his fault. If he weren't so... *Caring? Protective?* My mind taunts with unabashed glee.

"Can we discuss this later? Grim and I need to chat." Raising my brows in a pleading expression, they all nod before watching me drag Grim back outside. I'm not sure where this assertive Amelie came from—I've never dragged any man anywhere—but I'm not going to question my sudden audacity.

A light summer breeze barely cools the stress sweat coating my skin, and for the millionth time this week, I wish it was autumn already.

"Your friends didn't know about your dancing?"

Dropping my hold on Grim's wrist, I sink into the porch swing and cross my arms over my chest. "No, they didn't."

"Why not? Ashamed?"

"Not exactly." I consider how to explain the mixed emotions that have become my norm since creating my Velvet Venus persona. "It took a lot of courage to audition for Burlesque Night. I deal with anxiety, and one wrong move can cause my body to be dysregulated, but I love dancing. Dance classes were my life starting around five years old, but I dropped out around high school because I didn't look like the other girls, and my teacher wasn't exactly encouraging." The memory of Miss Shaw criticizing my weight is burned into my psyche, no matter how many therapy sessions I attend.

It's a freaking core memory—a blue orb like from that *Inside Out* movie.

"So, once Georgia hired me to perform, that was a huge leap for me. Taking another big step, like telling my friends, overwhelmed me, so I kept it to myself. It's not so much that I feared their judgment but worried about combining these two separate parts of me. Like if my real life collided with the hidden one, then the real Amelie's insecurities would take over."

Grim moves to sit beside me, his longer legs pushing the swing back and forth. "You talk as if both sides aren't you. Like they're not the real Amelie, but that's not true."

A chuckle of doubt bursts free. "You don't know me very well yet. You have no idea who the real me is."

"Maybe... or perhaps you're just underestimating yourself. Do you have any idea how fucking sexy you were on that stage? And it's not just your gorgeous curves either. You've got talent. My sister obviously recognized it if she hired you, then made sure I watched your performance."

"Georgia's your sister?" I don't know why I never made the connection before, but now that he's said it, the familiarity between their facial features is obvious.

Grim nods. "Yup, she's the brains in our partnership. So, trust me when I tell you not to sell yourself short. Burlesque Night is Georgia's baby, and she wouldn't put it in the hands of someone she didn't think had what it takes to make it successful. It's not like you interviewed in character, right? You impressed her just by being you first."

He has a point.

One I hadn't considered.

I'd attributed my ballsy attitude to Velvet Venus—faking it until I made it, so to speak. Like I'd been an imposter who managed to fool Georgia into believing I wasn't a reserved and nervous woman, rather than accepting I had more strength and confidence than I gave myself credit for.

"You're pretty wise, you know that? The club should have named you Yoda."

"I'll pitch it at the next club meeting," he teases, wrapping an arm across the back of the swing and my shoulders. "Are you feeling okay, otherwise? Not nauseous or anything?"

"No, I'm good. There was no need to worry."

He hugs me closer to his side, and I revel in the firm muscles of his chest and the faint whiff of his cologne. It reminds me of our kiss and how close we were last night. How I want to experience the same thing again.

"Not sure I can help it, babe." Grim toys with a strand of my hair, twirling it around his finger. "Logically, I figured you were alright. But with Georgia panicking over the club being short-staffed due to illness tonight, and the fact that you could be sick and no one know about it... I went a little crazy."

"Ya think?" My messages inbox is full of his frantic texts. Then something else occurs to me. "How did you get my number? From Snow and Caroline?"

Grim groans and rubs his free hand down his beard. "I stole it from your personnel file."

"Why?" Even with his explanation about half the club being sick, it's hard to understand why I matter so much. Sure, we kissed. It was hot. Passionate. And maybe he'd acted jealous over men watching me dance, and thinking Winston and I were an item, but all of those things still have trouble combating the lessons I've learned growing up perpetually single.

I'm too boring to capture and hold the interest of a man.

Men don't see me.

So why does *this* man—a badass ex-military biker—care so much? Is it because of Velvet Venus? He may say I'm both the seductress and the unassuming mouse, but what if that's all talk?

What if he thinks the woman who goes on stage every Tuesday is the kind of confident woman who'll fit perfectly into the Reaper's Wolves MC versus the quiet girl who uses a space heater in the summer because her anxiety is so bad?

CHAPTER EIGHT

GRIM

Amelie is thinking too hard. Doubting herself too much. And I fucking hate that life has taught her to question when someone compliments her or wants to ensure her safety.

"Why do I get the feeling that whatever I say, you'll have an excuse for why it's wrong?"

"Maybe you know me better than I think," she grumbles, and I can't help a half-grin at the adorable note of frustration in her voice.

"Glad you're catching on. But seriously, I don't have a list of rational reasons why I feel the way I do. I just know that ever since you sat next to me at the vet's office, I haven't been able to get you out of my head, and the fact that you showed up dancing at my club means something."

She mumbles under her breath. Something sounding a lot like *heart sparks*.

"You believe in that legend?" Suitor's Crossing loves to tout their myth about soulmates and love—*heart sparks*. Even our club president fell for it, or rather, fell for Caroline. Frankly, I haven't thought much about it either way, but perhaps something as elusive as soulmates is what's happening here, even if it sounds far-fetched.

"They're real for Caroline and Snow," Amelie echoes my thoughts, "But I would never presume that's what you feel for me, considering how long we've known each other. A freaking nanosecond."

"And yet, I know the sweet taste of your tongue tangling with mine." Her facial expressions are difficult to read under the moonlight, but I'd bet money she's blushing.

"Right... I'll work on accepting whatever this is." She waves her hand between us and then switches to a different, less intimate topic. "How did you end up working with your sister at Club Wolf?"

"I was already part of the Reaper's Wolves MC because Timber and I served together. When they were looking for someone to manage the club, I figured why not me? It was something to do since I'm not very mechanically savvy."

"What do you mean by that?"

"The MC also owns an auto body shop—it was the first business the club bought—but I suck at fixing cars, it makes no sense to me. Club Wolf was a better choice." I shrugged. "Anyway, Georgia had just graduated with her master's in business, and since our parents died two years ago, it's just me and her. She moved out here, convinced Snow to let her help me, and the rest is history."

When I list it all in a row, I realize how much my sister's dealt with the past few years. Major life changes from losing Mom and Dad to finishing post-grad to moving cross country. We don't usually deep dive into conversations about our feelings, but maybe it's time that changed. Time for me to check in on my headstrong sister instead of assuming she's doing fine.

"I'm sorry about your parents," Amelie says and rests her palm over my heart. "But it's amazing you guys get along well enough to work together, and that Georgia knew what she wanted to do at such a young age."

"Are you saying you struggled with learning what you wanted to do?" I latch onto the subject. Georgia can wait. This is my chance to learn more about the woman disrupting my previously routine life.

"Still struggling, actually," she admits. "I love dancing, but it's not a career option for me. One night of burlesque doesn't exactly pay the bills."

I pull Amelie's legs across my lap, readjusting her so her face isn't so hidden. "What about teaching? I'm sure dance studios are itching to have a talented woman like you leading classes."

Amelie throws her head back with a hearty laugh. "I doubt it. Besides, I'm pretty rusty, despite what you saw on Tuesday." A slight frown dims her features. Immediately, my protective instinct kicks into gear, ready to fight anyone who doesn't think Amelie's good enough.

She's a fucking goddess—on and off the stage.

Needing to erase her sadness, I warn her. "You're perfect, and I'm going to kiss you now."

Amelie jolts in my arms but doesn't push away at the declaration. Instead, her lashes flutter closed as her head drifts nearer, and I finally give in to the banked desire thickening my cock. Her plump thighs warm my lap. Rest right on top of my dick like a beacon tempting me to spread them wide and plow between them.

But I can't.

I won't.

Not here. Not like this.

Especially considering my caveman behavior from earlier.

All kinds of terrible scenarios filled my head when I tried to get a hold of Amelie and she didn't respond. Any regret over snooping through her file for her phone number and address had evaporated as images of Amelie sick and alone, with no one to care for her, made me nauseous with worry.

I didn't like the thought of her in pain, or by herself, so it'd been a relief when Snow had answered my call to let me know Amelie was in the clubhouse in Suitor's Crossing before I drove the hour to Everton.

A relief quickly followed by frustration, which is why I came in shouting, guns blazing, rather than calmly approaching the woman who'd been at the center of my concern. The group of guys who'd also been in the living area were probably having a field day sharing my erratic behavior with anyone on the compound who would listen.

Amelie moans as I nip her bottom lip, laving the tender flesh with my tongue soon after. My hand slides over her curves before landing on one heavy breast, squeezing the soft globe, anticipating the day when I'll get to see her tits in all their glory. Get to suck the prettiest nipples I bet I'll ever see.

"You're so sweet, little Amelie. How could I not worry about you?" My thumb strokes her cheek as I whisper in her ear, licking behind the sensitive shell.

"Grim..."

"Grayson," I correct. "You don't have to call me anything but Grayson."

"I like it," she breathes. "Your parents had a thing for 'G' names. Grayson and Georgia."

Unbidden, an image of our own child comes to mind, where I can continue the family tradition. *Damn, this woman really does have me fucked up in the head.*

Someone clears their throat in the background. What the hell? Can't they see I'm busy making out with my girl?

Amelie jerks back with a gasp and buries her face in my shoulder as I grit out a greeting, retribution in my eyes for the interruption. It's a new kid. So fresh from his last tour that his hair hasn't even outgrown its standard-issue buzzcut.

"Sorry to break up the party, but it looks like the flu isn't the only thing fucking with the club tonight. Your sister called when she couldn't get a hold of you."

"What did Georgia want?" I bark. My sister is a capable woman, plus she's got Timber and a couple of the other guys there to help her, so if she's still struggling, there must be a serious problem.

"They lost power."

"Excuse me?" Surely, he didn't say what I think he said. It's a clear sky, no thunderstorms, no excessive wind. "Why the hell would our power go out?"

"That's what she said." He shrugs his shoulders. "The power went out and you guys haven't installed generators yet. Because of that, combined with everyone being sick, Georgia decided to close down for the night to save the club's reputation. Everyone's getting drinks on the house the next time they come and their cover charge was refunded."

"Damn, that's gonna cost us." The club does extremely well but that's still a lot of money we're giving away to assuage our clients' annoyance. "Thanks for letting me know. I'll call Georgia later."

"Sure thing." Once he's gone, Amelie removes her legs from my lap and stands to stretch. "Well, I'm sure book club is wrapping up now, and it looks like you've got a fire to put out, so why don't we call it a night?"

Her nerves are back based on the fidgety way she keeps messing with her hair and bouncing her gaze between me and the front door. Like a hunted bunny searching for escape.

"This isn't how I envisioned tonight ending." I loop an arm around her waist and tuck her into my body, letting her feel the hard arousal hanging between my thighs.

"Another time," she gulps.

"You can count on it, baby." Pressing another kiss to her lips, I let her go back inside to say goodbye to her friends while I pulled my phone out to call Georgia.

What the hell is going on with the club recently? It's like I helped Alaska and Timber renovate the gym and somehow the club has gone to shit since, and I know it's not Georgia's fault. But what are the odds that all these little mishaps keep happening one after the other?

Suddenly, something clicks inside my head.

What *are* the odds? Maybe these are more than coincidences.

Deciding to get Ollie, our tech guy, involved, I redirect my steps to go find him. We can check our cameras to see if anything suspicious has been happening to coincide with these weird setbacks.

I don't know why anybody would want to sabotage Club Wolf, but we've dealt with our haters in the past. Recently with Alaska's woman's overly zealous religious father and before that, a traitorous member of our club working with another MC to steal from us.

So, it's not out of the realm of possibility that somehow these accidents are related, even if they seem completely innocuous. It just really fucking sucks if that's the case. Because I know all of us are tired of dealing with vindictive assholes.

After all, the MC is meant to be a peace haven for veterans, not a siren's call for trouble.

CHAPTER NINE

AMELIE

"Burlesque, huh?"

Beth and I decided to grab lunch together in our favorite cafe, so I knew it was only a matter of time before she brought up the elephant in the room. "I'm surprised you waited this long to mention it. Even more shocking is that I haven't heard from Kat yet," I say.

"That's because she knows we're having lunch today. I'm supposed to call afterward to give her the dirty details." Beth holds her hands up innocently when I make a face. "Her words, not mine."

"Of course... Although, I guess it's better you than me." At least I'll only have to tell the story once and then I can let Beth relay the message to everyone else.

It's not cowardice exactly. I just hate having to repeat myself. Well, that and I'm not much of a talker normally anyway. That goes into my whole not responding to text messages problem, too.

Except I don't seem to have a problem speaking with Grayson.

It's strange.

Like I want him to know more about me, and I don't want to hide, even though he could break my heart if I let him get too close.

He's the first man to really notice me. Which sounds pathetic and like I'm settling for any man's attention, but the romantic in me feels like it was always meant to be this way.

I'm not settling. Grayson isn't a consolation prize for someone better. He's more than I ever hoped for myself. A man enamored with me right off the bat, no slow build-up to attraction.

We unwrap our sandwiches, and I break open my bag of Doritos as I contemplate where to start. "You know I used to dance growing up."

"Until your teacher told you to give it up." Beth rolls her eyes. "Totally supportive and how you're supposed to treat your students, right?"

I silently agree, and Grayson's suggestion of me teaching dance classes floats to mind again. I dismissed it when he initially brought it up, but maybe there's something to it. After all, I know exactly how *not* to treat dancers yearning for encouragement and direction.

"I've always kind of regretted quitting, despite knowing I was never going to spin it into a career. Even before Miss Shaw crushed my dreams." I joke. "When Caroline mentioned Club Wolf a couple of months ago, I was curious about the place. Wondered what an upscale lounge run by leather-clad bikers would look like. While I was snooping on their website, I saw the Burlesque Night announcement, and it stuck in my head. I couldn't shake it."

Dreams of dancing again had taken over my life. I binged *Burlesque* multiple times. Played the soundtrack on repeat. Doing something so daring, so sexy, and uncharacteristic for me, became an addicting possibility.

"I dusted off my dancing shoes, so to speak, and auditioned to be one of their performers. And I got the gig."

"That is amazing. I'm so proud of you... and impressed by your bravery."

"Trust me, I don't feel brave ninety percent of the time. Honestly, that night after I auditioned, I had one of the worst panic attacks I've had in a while. Just worrying about making a fool of myself for nothing if I didn't get the job. Questioning who I thought I was after seeing all the other girls who were also there. It wasn't good."

"I wish you would have called. I would have come over." Beth reaches across the table to squeeze my arm.

"Thanks, but it wouldn't have helped. When I get to that place, I'd rather just be alone." Self-isolation is one of my biggest coping mechanisms, though not always the healthiest.

"I understand. Just know that I'm here for you if you ever need me, okay?" Beth continues after taking a bite of her sandwich. "So, you became an awesome burlesque dancer at Club Wolf, and that's how you met Grim?"

"Actually, we met the day before at the veterinarian's office."

"Really?"

"Yeah, Mabel freaked me out because of this bump on her back, which turned out to be nothing, thank goodness." *Another painful evening and morning of nerves for nothing*, I muse, remembering how anxious I felt. "I had an emergency appointment on my lunch break. There was only one chair left in the waiting room, and it was right next to Grim and his pit bull Tiny."

"Talk about an unexpected meet-cute. That the two of you would run into each other outside of the club you both work at. Actually, that you would run into each other outside of the Reaper's Wolves compound. We've been over there a ton."

"I know, right? I mean, I've seen Grim before from afar. But it's not like we've ever spoken before."

"Until now..." Beth sing-songs.

"Yep, and apparently he likes me." I bite into a crunchy chip waiting for her response.

"Of course he does. You're an intelligent, talented, and gorgeous woman. Don't act so surprised by it."

"I know I should feel more confident considering Caroline and Faith both snagged their own hot biker. But it just seems so out of reach for me. Like, *well, of course, great guys fell for them.* They're beautiful and smart."

"And so are you."

"Logically, I know that's true, but it doesn't seem possible in reality."

Beth sighs and leans back in her chair, playing with the scrapped pieces of her straw wrapper. "I feel the same way."

"Oh? Is there someone who's caught your eye?" Beth blushes and avoids answering by snagging her drink and sucking up the pink lemonade. "Oh my gosh, there is. Who is it?"

I rack my brain to remember if I've seen her around any other MC members, but no one comes to mind. The only one I'm positive it *isn't* is Timber because we all see the way he looks at Lindy, even if she keeps denying there's anything between them.

"We're not talking about me. We're talking about you," Beth deflects.

"I'm gonna let this slide for now." I understand someone wanting to keep something to themselves. Heck, it's what I'd probably still be doing if Grayson hadn't barged into the compound and called me out about the club. "But only because I understand the need to have a secret that's just yours."

"Like your burlesque dancing was supposed to be."

"I liked keeping it as just my own thing. I mean, most of it was fear. Irrational fear, because I knew you guys would support me. But I also liked the secret identity part of it."

"The intoxicating adventure of living a double life," Beth teases, and I contemplate her words as we finish lunch.

The intoxicating part of my double life was the fact that I had the nerve to even have one. That I didn't have to be boring Amelie all the time. I could slip into a sexier, more confident persona who naturally lived an exciting life. But if my two selves were merging now, perhaps I didn't need the illusion of Velvet Venus being a separate entity from me.

Like Grayson said.

These past few months have been anything but boring. They've been bold and invigorating. From my burlesque to my biker.

A shock rolls through my system at the realization.

It may seem naive, but I've kept Velvet Venus and Amelie Swanson in two boxes for so long that I considered them separate and vastly different people. There was a disconnect.

But Velvet Venus is Amelie.

She is me.

And it doesn't matter if no one—particularly men—ever noticed her before because it doesn't negate her existence. Doesn't negate the truth.

Goosebumps run down my arms as my breathing picks up. I feel like I'm having an epiphany of massive proportions but have no clue how to deal with it.

Talk to your therapist.

Let her help you work through this.

And so I do, with a message sent asking for an impromptu therapy session as Beth switches to a different topic and we finish our lunches, my thoughts racing to figure out what this means for my future.

CHAPTER TEN

GRAYSON

"You think somebody is intentionally sabotaging Club Wolf?" Snow asks from his position at the head of the conference table. I decided to voice my suspicions at our club meeting to make everyone aware of the possibility of someone fucking with our businesses again.

"Possibly," I hedge. "A string of accidents like we've had doesn't seem entirely coincidental, especially when they're affecting our bottom line. Georgia told me one of our VIP guests canceled a reservation for Saturday night due to a colleague's poor experience last week when we were short-staffed."

"Ollie, let's check the security footage and see what we find. Hopefully, nothing." Snow runs a hand through his hair. "But if it's Breaker and his crew again, he will regret reneging on our truce."

A rumble of agreement arcs across the room as the rest of the guys nod and mentally prepare for a possible showdown. Unlike most MCs, we're legit. We don't have turf wars per se, but we also don't take shit from those that prefer to live outside the law. Like Breaker and the rest of the Ghost Rider MC.

"Timber, let's add you to security at the club until we figure this out. If we need to beef things up to keep everyone safe, don't hesitate to take care of it."

I'm thankful Timber and I will be working together again. He's one of our best mechanics at the body shop, so we haven't really been a team since our Army days, but with him at my back, whatever's going down at Club Wolf should get shut down quickly.

Which is exactly what I need if Amelie's going to continue to dance there.

The possessive beast inside me wants to lock her away so no one else gets a peek at her curvy body, but the rational—albeit *hanging onto his rationality by a thread*—man understands that she's a grown woman who can make decisions for herself.

I still hate it, though.

Especially when another Tuesday night rolls around and Amelie is back again.

She swivels her hips in a slow roll as the men nearest the stage whistle and shout obscene pick-up lines. A tension headache builds in my temples the longer I grind my teeth and watch the show from the sidelines. My palms are going to have permanent nail marks from my fists squeezing so tight in an effort not to end up in the middle of some bastard's face.

Finally, Amelie finishes with a wink and shimmy before bouncing off stage with extra enthusiasm. "I think this is the largest crowd we've had yet." Sweat shines on her forehead and cleavage as she grabs my arm and turns to look out at the audience. Not that we can see much with the stage lights blinding us.

"I don't like it."

"What do you mean you don't like it? More customers are good for business."

"I don't like so many men getting a view of your body. I should be the only man you dance for," I remind her, needing reassurance that she's mine.

We went bowling over the weekend as our first date and tried to bring our relationship down to a reasonable level. You know, one where I'm not already completely obsessed with her.

The date was fun, but it failed its purpose. Because all I want to do is speed ahead, not slow down.

"A private dance could be arranged..." The drawled suggestion is shy but beneath the initial hesitancy lies curiosity. Desire.

Immediately, I drag her to one of the two private rooms we keep for small parties—for those who need complete anonymity versus the social status of our VIP second-level. Both rooms are empty tonight since the burlesque dancers don't entertain men by themselves, unlike our regular exotic dancers, which makes it the perfect place for me to finally get another taste of Amelie.

I lock the door with my master key and recline on the black leather sofa facing a raised dais and gleaming silver pole. Pointing toward the set-up, I growl, "Consider it arranged. Dance for me, little goddess."

"But... I don't have the rest of my costume. There's nothing else to take off." She gestures to her cropped corset and high-waisted panties. Today she played the role of a Southern Belle, complete with a frilly parasol and hoop skirt.

Pressing a button hidden behind the couch, I shake my head and smirk. *My sweet innocent Amelie.* "Looks to me that you still have plenty of clothing to lose. And only for me, too."

Amelie gapes at the suggestion before tilting her head to the side, contemplating my challenge. Will she accept it? Trust me not to abuse her vulnerability?

She licks her lips and takes one step forward, then another, until the slow strobe lights overhead paint her curves in blue and purple.

"Pole dancing is a different style from my usual," she warns. Her fingers wrap around the bar and I imagine the feel of them closing around my cock. My hand drops to adjust my growing erection, and Amelie's gaze hones in on the motion, riveted by the sight of the obvious bulge along my left leg.

"You'll figure something out... I have complete faith that your body knows exactly how to ride a pole." She can't miss the insinuation, and I swear the heat of her embarrassment-soaked arousal washes over me from here.

The chorus of an R&B song croons in the background as Amelie begins a tentative circle around the stage. She allows her body to lean outward, her hair swinging down in a seductive swish, and lets her eyes close for a moment, feeling the music.

"Eyes on me, gorgeous."

Like a good girl, her lashes flick open to reveal blown pupils as Amelie continues to put on the sexiest fucking show I've ever had the pleasure of watching.

She may doubt her talent or appeal, but there is absolutely no fucking evidence to support that belief.

"You're beautiful, Amelie. I knew you wouldn't disappoint me."

Far from it.

Even if tonight ends with this, both of us still clothed after a sensual dance, it'll be enough. Be worth the case of blue balls I'll be going home with.

Amelie dips low, popping her ass out and I groan when her panties stretch to cover the round cheeks.

And that's when she decides to bring the party to me. By crawling on her goddamn hands and knees. Like a sleek jungle cat in heat.

Pre-cum soaks my boxer briefs. Loosening my belt and jeans, I fist my cock through the cotton.

"Is that for me?" Amelie asks with a lick of her lips.

How the hell does this woman have any doubts about her body and attraction?

"Only for you."

A sly grin accompanies a leisurely climb into my lap, grinding her panty-covered pussy onto my aching cock.

"Is this what you wanted?" she whispers, leaning forward to brush a kiss over my cheek and then ear. "A lap dance?"

"I want whatever you'll give me, little goddess. Tonight, I worship at your altar. Prepared to give you whatever you need. So take it. Ride my cock with that sweet pussy of yours and make yourself come."

My fingers find the zipper to her corset and draw the metal down to release her magnificent tits. They bounce and jiggle with every roll of her hips, and I can't stop myself from capturing one of the swollen buds with my lips, sucking hard.

Amelie mewls and quickens her pace, driving her body deeper into mine. I'm surrounded by soft pale skin. Smothered by gorgeous curves.

I'm in fucking heaven.

And when Amelie cries out, her body shuddering from pleasure, I finally allow myself to let go, shooting my seed past the brim of my boxers to drip down my stomach.

Our breaths are heavy. Music still plays in the background. Cupping the back of Amelie's head, I drag her closer for a kiss before admitting, "*You* are exactly what I want, baby."

CHAPTER ELEVEN

AMELIE

My freezing toes curl within the flats pressed close to the space heater again, though this time I can't tell if it's because of a misguided anxious part of me or just the air conditioner being extra icy today. Either way, I pray Jenna stays busy gossiping with Kelly, so my body has enough time to heat up before she says something.

If you were with Grim, this wouldn't be a problem.

The memory of our evening together elicits a quiet hum of contentment as a tingle of awareness blooms between my thighs.

Stop it! You can't think of sex while at work. Focus on something else.

If you taught dance, your toes and everything else wouldn't have time to get cold.

That's better. Safer. Dance over Grayson.

Besides, ever since the suggestion of teaching came up, my thoughts kept circling back to it. Dancing or teaching won't cure my anxiety, but having a job I love is bound to improve my mental health.

Will you love it?

It's not guaranteed since I've never taught a class in my life. It could be terrible. Worse than what I'm currently doing.

Maybe instead of diving into the deep end, I should take baby steps and test the waters.

Biting my lip, I grab my phone and text my cousin Natalie. She leases a studio in Suitor's Crossing for her yoga classes. Perhaps she'll let me host a free dance clinic or something to gauge interest—mine and the town's.

Of course, if it all works out, that means a move to Suitor's Crossing.

I'll be closer to Caroline, but further from Kat and Beth who live in Everton like me.

I'll also be closer to my extended family, Winston and Natalie.

My phone rings, and I immediately answer. "That was fast."

"When my favorite cousin mentions possibly switching careers, you bet your ass I'm gonna work fast. You could help me with the goats, I can learn some sexy dance moves, and we could be roommates. It's a win all around!" Natalie's excitement is catching even if everything is theoretical at this point.

"I'm not promising anything with the goats." One of her most popular classes is goat yoga with baby goats prancing around the studio and climbing on clients. "But I like the sound of being roommates. You've always been the sister I never had."

A flurry of click-clacks sounds in the background before Natalie says, "There's a Saturday free next week if you want to use it. We can spread the word about inclusive dance classes that welcome people of all sizes and talent levels. Oh! Maybe it can be like an informal dance party where you show us some moves, and we can have Buttercream Dreams bake some cute cupcakes and..."

Natalie continues spit-balling ideas while I envision a group of young men and women finding a safe place to express themselves in a class under my tutelage—a contrast to what I grew up with.

It sounds amazing. And terrifying.

Who do I think I am slapping the title of "Dance Instructor" on my chest and charging people for my guidance? Do I even know the first thing about starting my own business? Because that's what this would be. My own dance academy. My responsibility. From marketing to teaching to freaking health insurance for my medications.

"What the hell am I thinking, Nat?" I interrupt her rambling about what to call the evening. Another chill breaks out over my entire body, crackling through my calves and stomach like an iceberg emerging from the ocean.

"That you're a capable young woman who's tired of denying your dreams." Natalie pauses. "I know you didn't grow up dreaming of instructing students, but you *did* grow up dreaming of dancing—especially after you quit. Pursuing this is a good thing. Even if this is just a one-time deal because you learn you hate it. You'll have pushed yourself out of your comfort zone, which is always a positive."

"You don't think I'm being irresponsible or ridiculous by believing anyone would want to learn from me? Miss Chubby Thighs?" That's what some of the girls used to call me in dance class. Snickering behind their lithe limbs and flat stomachs.

"Those are assets. Trust me, there are people like you who would love to take a dance class but fear judgment. You'll be doing them a service."

Well, when she put it like that...

"Seriously? Get warmer socks. It's like the seventh ring of hell in here," Jenna calls from over the cubicle wall.

"Sorry, Nat. I gotta go, but we'll talk later." I hang up and apologize to Jenna before turning off the heater.

"You'd think with all that stuffing you'd be sweltering in this heat... Miss Chubby Thighs." Jenna smirks. Obviously, she overheard my conversation with Natalie, and twin flames of embarrassment stained my cheeks.

I do *not* need her to start bullying me.

Ignoring the insult, I refocus on work, but in the back of my mind, plans for the future begin swirling into a tornado of change.

"WHAT DO YOU THINK?"

Grayson and I are at a dog park in Suitor's Crossing with Tiny and my cousin's dogs, Gremlin and Farrah. The three pups have run into each other at the vet's office so often that they're good friends, which makes for a fun playdate—for them and us.

It's nice to see Grayson outside of the Reaper's Wolves compound and Club Wolf. An air of tension permeated both since he shared his concerns over someone intentionally sabotaging the club. Though I have my doubts about it. Everyone I've met during Burlesque Night has been friendly, not exactly the type to commit petty crimes like cutting power to the entire building by fraying a few wires.

But that's what confirmed Grayson's suspicions. He didn't believe they frayed on their own.

"It sounds like a solid plan." He lightly squeezes my hand as we continue to stroll around the perimeter of the park. I didn't expect such a big gruff guy like Grayson to be into hand-holding, but the moment our feet hit the pavement after arriving he snagged my hand with his and didn't let go.

It's sweet.

And butterfly-inducing.

Like we're a real couple, and this isn't a passing fling for him.

"Really? Natalie and the girls think so, too, but I'm still pretty nervous. Say we throw this introductory dance party and no one shows up? It'll be like my twelfth birthday party all over again."

"No one went to your twelfth birthday party?" We stopped to pet our three furry terrors, who decided to check on us before running back across the green field full of other dogs.

"Nope. It was humiliating." Just the memory of it is enough to induce a shudder. "Someone started a rumor that the date had changed, so nobody showed up at the park. That's always kind of stuck with me, despite knowing it was just some little kid's idea of a prank. I'm sure it contributes to my less-than-perfect mental health."

"Stop putting yourself down," he gently scolds. "Plus, I guarantee at least one person will be at your event. Me. Tiny, too, if he's allowed."

I laugh, warm contentment settling in my belly. For a guy who thinks in worst-case scenarios, he certainly doesn't let me get away with doing the same thing. It makes me want to encourage him as much as he does me. "If goats are allowed in that studio, I don't see what the problem with dogs would be."

"That's right, your cousin does the goat yoga."

"Yep..." The summer sun shines brightly as we step out from under a copse of trees, and a couple of Golden Retrievers are snapping at the dandelions floating on a soft breeze. It's idyllic, and I'm grateful Grayson called and asked if I'd like to join him today. Especially since I know how busy he's been lately. "How are things going at the club now that there's an official investigation going on?"

"The security cameras haven't found anything suspicious yet. Whoever is doing this has a good idea of where the blind spots are."

I frown, bewildered by the potential ramifications of such knowledge. "An inside job? That doesn't sit right with me."

"Considering Georgia and I both vet our new hires, I agree. But it's the only thing that makes sense." He stops us under a shady tree a few minutes later and turns to stroke my cheek, his serious eyes blazing with promise. "Don't worry, though. We'll catch whoever this is, and I will personally be ensuring your safety."

The breath hitches in my lungs. "Is that necessary? None of the accidents have affected me."

"Yet," he adds. "And I'm going to keep it that way." His lips brush across mine in finality, stopping any argument from me. Not that I planned on pushing back too hard. Personal protection from my very own military veteran? A rough-riding MC biker?

Yes, please.

CHAPTER TWELVE

AMELIE

After leaving the park and dropping Gremlin and Farrah off with Winston, we return to Grayson's room at the compound. I park beside his truck as he helps Tiny get down from the steep drop of the passenger side to the ground.

"Have you ever thought about getting one of those sidecars you can attach to your motorcycle so Tiny can still go everywhere with you? He'd be super cute with a mini helmet and goggles."

A shout of laughter bellows from his chest as he pets Tiny's head then rounds the truck, taking my hand and leading me inside the clubhouse. "They're more of a novelty item, but now you've got me considering getting one just for fun. Tiny would fucking love it."

"Me, too. Count on me to take all of the pictures."

"How do you plan on doing that when you'll be riding with me on the back of my bike, babe?" His teasing smile has me ducking my head as a flush of pleasure rushes forward. As soon as we're inside the clubhouse, Tiny races across the living room and hops on the couch, snuggling into Timber's lap.

"Sometimes I think he likes you better than me," Grayson says with an exasperated sigh.

Timber smiles and continues to scratch behind Tiny's ears. "Of course he does. He knows I've always got a treat waiting for him, don't you, boy?" And true to his word, a small bone-shaped treat appears in his hand before quickly disappearing with a swipe of Tiny's tongue.

Grayson huffs. "You spoil him." But there's no heat behind his words. With a wave, we bypass the living area and head upstairs. "Sorry, I don't have a private cabin like some of the other guys. I've never seen the need for it as one person."

"No problem. It's kind of like college again." With shared bathrooms and communal spaces like the kitchen and living room, it hadn't occurred to me exactly how much the compound resembled dorm living until now.

But not in a negative way.

These guys are used to living in shared quarters from their time serving in the military, and here they've recreated a close-knit community. Although I live in an apartment, I couldn't tell you who my neighbors are. We hardly see each other. Here it's different. Kind of cozy.

Something I never thought I'd say about a biker compound.

"You're not far off," Grayson says, studying the space as if for the first time. It's neat except for a couple of tees tossed on a dresser rather than folded in the drawers. Framed photos of him with a group of serious-looking men decorate one wall while a window offers a view of the mountains.

"Except you have way more space than my single room had, although I'm guessing the same could be said for the guys' dorm. Honestly, I never ventured over there, so this is a first."

Grayson smirks at my admission.

"Don't look too smug about it." I cover my face and frown. It's embarrassing to be a virgin in every sense of the word. Embarrassing to admit to the hot guy who's probably never had a problem finding partners that this is my first time in a man's room. First time anywhere near a man's bed.

"Hey, it's nothing to be ashamed about." He gently removes my hands from my face and kisses my palms.

"Technically, I know that. Doesn't stop the humiliation, though."

We haven't been alone together like this since the night I danced for him at the club. The night I came against his cock in nothing more than my panties. Lust hits me hard in the gut then slides lower, forcing me to press my thighs together for a little pressure against my clit.

That was the single hottest night of my life.

I felt empowered. Feminine. Like the goddess, Grayson calls me.

"You can't make that sound while we're in here, gorgeous," the gravelly tone of his voice puts me on edge. It's the same one he used at the club when he ordered me to dance for him.

"What sound?"

He backs me up against his raised mattress and lightly circles my throat with his palm. "That one. That sexy little hum you make right here." His thumb taps the center of my esophagus. "The one that says you're thinking of me doing unspeakably filthy things to you."

"What if that's what I want? There's no shame in being a virgin, but it's not something I've been holding onto for any particular reason." I swallow hard. Too desperate for Grayson to question my boldness.

There's a need inside me. Always has been. But I've denied it time and time again because it only appeared when I was alone imagining my dream man.

The way he'd touch me.

The way he'd love me.

Grayson is that man. Even if this isn't forever, I want this—*him*—right now. I want him to be my first. And if he ends up being my only, then my romantic heart will be happy. But for now, my greedy body is ruling my actions, and it needs to be dominated by this burly biker and his big dick.

"You don't know what you're asking for, gorgeous." His lips feather over my jaw to whisper in my ear. "I want to use you. You've teased and tempted me every time you stepped on stage at Club Wolf, and I let you hold the reins when this hot pussy rode my dick." One hand drops to cup me through my shorts, punctuating his point.

"But now it's my turn, and I'm not sure you're ready. Virgins require gentle touches. Patience."

"Not this one." I force his hand deeper between my thighs, needing him to understand how much my desire matches his. "I'm not an eighteen-year-old girl nervous about losing her virginity after prom. I'm a thirty-three-year-old woman who's read her fair share of erotica and has a healthy self-care routine. Hearts and flowers are nice. Soft and slow has its place. But I'm telling you that it's not here. Not now."

Anticipation blooms in the air as he studies my stubborn, and hopefully convincing, expression. This is more forthright than I've ever been with my desires before. But ever since my epiphany about the confident Velvet Venus being me, rather than a separate entity, I've been reevaluating things.

My therapist spoke of false beliefs and dimming my light, and it put into question everything I thought about myself. For years, I've described myself as shy, boring, too chubby, and too quiet—reasons why I never had a boyfriend or fit into the popular crowd.

And at one point, those things might have been true.

But why am I still holding onto them? So, I'm reserved, work in a cubicle, and spend most of my free time reading. Those don't negate the fact that I also love to dance, revel in showing off my curves to an audience, and live an interesting life.

Those beliefs aren't serving me anymore.

They're not protecting me; they're hindering me.

Stopping me from accepting my full self because all the parts of me don't fit neatly together in a socially acceptable way. If you're shy, you can't also like performing for the public. If you're quiet, you can't also be comfortable voicing an opinion.

Society loves labels, and my anxious brain does, too, but it's time I relax and just let myself be.

Starting now.

"If at any time, you want to stop, say the word," Grayson says, fiery resolve igniting in his eyes. "But if we're doing this, you need to be a lot more naked."

Nodding eagerly, I help him tug off my shirt and bra then kick off my shoes and shorts until I'm left standing in my panties. Self-consciousness briefly peeks its head up before I slam it down with a mallet like in a game of Whack-a-mole.

"Lay down on the bed with your head near the side here." He pats the right side of the mattress, and as I obey his command, he swiftly rids himself of everything but a pair of black boxer briefs.

Good lord. The man is packing in every sense of the word. Thick cock tenting his briefs. Burly chest rising and falling with heavy breaths. Tree-trunk thighs flexing with strength each time he moves.

He's a warrior through and through, and I'm the lucky woman he's chosen to ravage.

Grayson rounds the bed and tilts my chin up so my head hangs over the edge of the mattress. It's a vulnerable position. My body is laid out before him in a scrap of flimsy lace while my neck is stretched from the gravity pulling my head downward.

Roughened fingertips trail over the ridges of my throat before cupping my chin. His thumb presses on my bottom lip, drawing it slightly open. "This is how I want to fuck your mouth, little goddess," he murmurs, the husky admission causing my heart rate to skyrocket. He slides his thumb between my lips to land on my tongue. "My cock filling this pretty mouth until you're choking on it. Then you'll take me deeper, won't you, baby?"

God, yes. I moan and nod. What he is describing should scare me. Freak me out.

Choking has never featured high in my fantasies, but Grayson makes the act sound sexy. Has me arching my neck to get closer to the bulge behind the minimal amount of fabric separating us. A bulge directly in front of me.

"I knew you were secretly a bad girl." He chuckles before removing his hand from my face and tugging his briefs lower, kicking them off once they fall to his feet. His heavy dick bobs with the motion, and I catch a glimpse of metal shining underneath the mushroom head.

No way.

How did I miss a piercing when I climbed into his lap and grinded myself to orgasm on his cock?

"Is that..." I reach a hand up to capture his erection for closer inspection, but Grayson makes a *tsking* sound with his tongue and catches my wrist.

"No hands, baby. Not yet." Both of my arms are drawn up high above my chest, clasped together at the wrists with one of his large palms. "This is all about you trusting me. Giving me control because you want to please me. I say what goes. Understand?"

"Yes."

"Good girl," he rumbles in approval, and another gush of arousal slicks my thighs. Grayson taps his cock on my lips once, twice, before ordering me to open for him. I eagerly obey, and he rewards me by slipping the wide head an inch inside my mouth.

"Remember, if you want me to stop, I will. Just tap out, okay?" He releases my hands and manually pats his hip with my palm to remind me that I'm safe with him. That I ultimately call the shots. And my jaw opens more to suck him deeper, needing to show him my appreciation for his protective nature.

"Fuck, baby, you really want my cock, don't you?" Grayson's large palms grasp either side of my head and massage the scalp as he presses forward. Inch by slow inch he fills my mouth until he bumps the back of my throat, causing me to choke a little.

"Breathe through your nose, Amelie. You can do this. You're already doing so well." The praise melts into me. I've always been a sucker for encouragement. Words of affirmation. And when it comes from Grayson? It's all the more potent.

Saliva slicks his entry as he quickens his thrusts. Obscene, wet sucking sounds block everything else out, and I can't resist touching my body in response. Playing with my nipples. Toying with my sensitive clit.

This is so fucking dirty.

Letting Grayson fuck my mouth until I'm choking around his fat dick. Until tears and spit spill down my cheeks. I feel so dirty and so fucking good. Like the baddest bitch in Suitor's Crossing.

And it's a wild sensation.

I would never use those words to describe myself or any other woman. They're usually derogatory terms, but in this case, they feel powerful and transformative. Suddenly, I understand a little bit about degradation kinks and why people like them if they feel anything like this.

"I'm about to come, babe. Are you ready for me? I'm going to fill this hot mouth with my cum, and you're going to swallow it all like a good girl, aren't you?"

There's no way he can expect an answer when my mouth is otherwise occupied, so I just stare up at him and squeeze his hips with my fingers, praying he understands the silent communication.

One more thrust and Grayson roars his release, spilling down my throat and overflowing my mouth to drip down my cheeks, mixing with my tears and spit. My muscles work to swallow as much of him as I can before he pulls out and falls to his knees. Tender kisses travel from my neck to my lips, and I'm kind of shocked Grayson wants to kiss me right now.

"Fuck, Amelie. What am I going to do with you?"

"Don't make me wait any longer," I gasp. My fingers frantically work my clit, but it's not enough. I want to feel Grayson stretching me open. Want to feel his firm body rubbing against mine.

"As if I could." He circles the bed and climbs over my prone form. He lines his cock up with my pussy entrance then pins my hands to the mattress. "You're soaking the comforter, gorgeous. Already so wet for me just from sucking my cock. Such a naughty girl." His hips slam forward, and I scream in shocked pleasure.

I thought he'd go slow again, tease me with incremental thrusts before burying himself deep. Need more time to recover from his release.

How wrong I was.

"Grayson!" I cry out, my thighs clamping around his waist as he sets a punishing pace.

"This is what you wanted, isn't it, little goddess? You wanted to be fucked. This sexy little body craves it." His teeth bite at a nipple, already stiff and aching from my ministrations, and another splash of wetness coats his cock in response.

Damn, our book club teases Caroline for being the kinkiest out of all of us, but I'm thinking we've got it wrong. Because I never imagined I'd be into such rough sex. Choking. Biting. It always seemed out of place during a time when a couple was supposed to be pleasuring the other.

But I underestimated the power of pleasure-pain.

And why not? It's not like I ever had anything to compare it to. I either experienced pleasure or pain—not an addicting mixture of both. Until Grayson.

"More," I beg, digging my heels into his ass and scratching at his back. That metal piercing keeps hitting my G-spot, building the tension in my limbs with each powerful plunge of Grayson's cock, until everything bursts in blinding light. Searing sparks of euphoria rain down as I fight to catch my breath.

Grayson's orgasm isn't too far behind, his body collapsing onto mine after a few more seconds. Our pounding hearts beat next to each other. Our breathing synchronizes as one.

"How do you feel, gorgeous?"

With my eyes closed, I take stock of myself.

Satisfied. Happy. Whole.

And something else. Something I know is equally important to Grayson as it is to me. So as we slowly come down from our high, I hug him close and whisper, "Safe."

CHAPTER THIRTEEN

GRAYSON

The sunrise will soon edge over the mountains, and the best night of my life will officially end. Of course, Amelie is still snuggled next to me in my bed, but eventually, she'll have to go home, while I deal with whatever is happening at Club Wolf. Though, honestly, I feel too good at the moment to give much of a fuck about work.

What I really want to do is keep Amelie locked away with me today. To continue exploring this explosive chemistry between us. To learn more about the conundrum that is my shy but brave girl.

But since that's out of the question, I'll make the most out of the little bit of time we have left this morning. Slipping under the comforter, I place gentle kisses down her spine and over a round hip, remembering my harsh grip there hours earlier, when I fucked her from behind after recovering from our first round of sex.

Tenderly, I roll Amelie to her back and spread her legs wider with my shoulders. I got a taste of her last night after sucking her arousal off my fingers, but I'm ready to drink straight from the source. She smells like us—a salty sweet musk—and her folds are still puffy from being taken so roughly.

Don't worry, baby, I'll take care of you.

My tongue sweeps across her tender flesh, licking her tight opening and sensitive clit. I imagine the pink of her pussy deepening to a darker color as her subconscious reacts to my kisses, and I wish I could witness the change for myself. But flipping off the covers means exposing Amelie to the cool air of the bedroom, and that's not how I want to wake her up.

With an icy shock to her system.

No, my little goddess deserves to be *loved* awake. Worshiped enough to rise and begin her day completely satisfied.

A quiet moan sounds from above as Amelie shifts, instinctively raising her hips for more. *My pleasure.* Burying my face deeper between her thighs, I return to giving her long, languorous licks to ease her into an orgasm rather than speeding toward completion with firmer strokes.

"Mmm... Grayson," Amelie murmurs, one of her hands sliding beneath the sheets to find my head and massage the short strands of hair.

"Good morning, gorgeous," I breathe against her clit before sucking the firm bud between my lips. She jolts at the contact, her legs fidgeting on either side of my body as she tries to find relief.

Instantly, I trap her legs with my arms and hold her still. "Be good, baby. All that wiggling is interrupting my breakfast."

"But... I..." Her back arches as a rush of hot cream coats my tongue and chin. *Fuck, I could eat this sweet pussy all day.* Amelie's climax has barely subsided when I work her up to another one, this time with my mouth and fingers working in tandem to fuck and suck her little body to completion.

"No... I can't..."

"One more, baby. One more, then I'll let you rest," I promise, rolling her clit between my teeth for concentrated lashings of my tongue. That's all it takes to push her over the brink, and as soon as I ease the last drop of her orgasm free, I rise to kiss her good morning. "You're such a good girl for me. Coming for your man like that."

She murmurs sleepily as I cuddle her close to my chest. This woman is perfect for me. I can't get enough of her.

And it's with thoughts of our future together that I fall back asleep, knowing she's safe within my arms.

AN ADORABLE GIGGLE wakes me up a few hours later. This time the sun has fully risen and warm yellow light spills into the room. Amelie and I have switched positions, so she's hugging my back, making me the little spoon.

"What's so funny, gorgeous?"

"Me being the big spoon to your giant self," she says with another laugh before she rubs her cheek across my shoulder blade like a sleepy kitten.

Lifting one of her hands to my mouth for a brief kiss, I admit, "It's a nice change every once in a while. Do you not like it?"

"Oh no! I'll take any opportunity I can to clamp my arms around these big, hard muscles." Her clutch tightens. I groan and shift—my morning wood still disappointed about not getting a chance to sink into her wet heat after I ate her out at dawn—relishing the squish of her breasts and belly against my body.

"Careful..." Amelie's teeth suddenly sink into my skin with a playful bite. "A girl could get used to waking up like this."

"Wouldn't bother me one bit, babe." Because I know for a fact I'm already addicted to having her in my bed. "Are you always this feisty in the morning?"

"With you, I guess so. I'm just really happy and excited to start the day. Is that weird since we didn't exactly get much sleep last night?"

God, this woman is trying to kill me. All I want to do is make sure she stays happy. Ensure she greets each day with optimism and joy because she knows I've always got her back. I'll always protect and support her.

"Nope, not weird at all. Your dance event is this evening, which is the perfect reason to be eager for today. Anything to lessen your stress and anxiety—including the liberal use of orgasms—I'm going to do."

"Oh crap!" I feel Amelie jolt to a sitting position, and I quickly whip around, ready to solve whatever just changed.

"What? What's wrong?"

Reaching over me to her phone on the nightstand, she lights up the screen before shutting it back off. "It's almost 9 a.m. I've got to get home to take my meds on time. I don't want to take them late, especially today, when I need to be at my best."

I nod in immediate understanding and roll out of bed, grabbing tees and sweats for both of us to wear from my dresser. "Come on, I'll drive you, then we can grab breakfast together."

We're on the road ten minutes later, after I took Tiny out to pee and filled his bowl with kibble. "So, you said meds, plural," I say, curiosity getting the best of me. "I know about your anxiety, but is there something else, too? No judgment. I'd just like to know what you're comfortable telling me. In case there's ever a time I need to advocate for you or anything."

She shrugs as we navigate the winding road back to town. "Anxiety and acid reflux. Those are my current health issues. The reflux was diagnosed a couple of months ago after I kept waking up in the middle of the night feeling nauseous with this burning sensation in my throat."

"Fuck, that sounds intense."

"It was, but everything's a lot better now. I mean, I slept well last night."

"I'd like to think I had a hand in that." I grin and pat her thigh where my palm rests. Whenever I'm near Amelie a primal need rises to keep her close. To touch her in some way. "Thank you for sharing with me. I know discussing your health can be a bitch when so many people don't really understand what you're going through."

"True. But I'm fortunate enough to have family and friends who accept me as I am. Somehow I avoided getting parents whose ideas for solutions included exercising more or praying about it. Not that I don't think those things have their place, but I needed more, you know?"

Awe clamps around my heart. Amelie is so strong. So brave. But she would never admit it. She recognized that something wasn't right in her life and set out to get answers. To become a healthier, happier version of herself.

I know men from my military unit who still struggle to do the same work. Everyone moves at their own pace and timing, but damn... Amelie is a fucking warrior. A fucking goddess.

My girl is a warrior goddess, and the twelve-year-old boy inside me is fist-pumping in victory right now because I always had a crush on Xena from that old TV show.

I thought I was obsessed with Amelie before. Sexy. Shy. Smart and strong.

But now my obsession is cemented.

For good.

CHAPTER FOURTEEN

AMELIE

"**A**re you excited yet?" Natalie claps her hands in enthusiasm as she meets Grayson and me at the back door to the studio. It took us an hour to get here after taking my medicine and then grabbing breakfast pastries at Buttercream Dreams. The owner, Sierra, promised that everything is set for tonight since she's providing custom cookies for the event.

"It's unbelievable how quickly everything has come together." I can't help the wide smile tugging at my lips. Once my cousin gets an idea in her head, it's full steam ahead, and supporting my newfound dream is no different. She spent the past week helping me figure out a business plan while also spreading the word about tonight to anyone who would listen within a twenty-mile radius of Suitor's Crossing.

"When you've got a dream, why wait any longer than you have to to make it happen?"

"Good point."

Natalie unlocks the door and flips on the lights the further we walk down a hall leading to the main studio. "Winston said he'd be by later today to help out. He's got a couple of morning appointments to get through, and then he and Guin will be here."

"Awesome. Even if it's just us tonight, at least that's five people."

"Oh, it's going to be a lot more than five people," Natalie says, and I see Grayson nod his head in agreement. "I've been hyping you up to all of my yoga classes."

"And they seem excited?" It's still surprising to me that people are willing to take a chance on me. I'm a stranger. I'm not even local to Suitor's Crossing.

"Duh. That's what I've been telling you. Give the people what they need. Basic business principles."

"You would know," I say, bowing down to her expertise. I trust Natalie knows what she's doing after successfully running her yoga studio for five years. "Guess it's time we get to work, huh?"

We chose a neon 80s theme for the dance party to encourage participation since most people are familiar with that era of music and it's easy to have fun with. Winston and his wife arrive two hours later, and everyone splits up. The three of us women decorate the walls with streamers and party decor while the guys set up a couple of round tables at the edges of the room.

This isn't a traditional dance class since we're making it a sort of party mixer, but as things come together my nerves kick up.

This is becoming very real.

"Hey, are you doing okay?" Grayson's strong arms circle my waist as he braces my back, letting me sink into him, and I'm thankful for his support. He hasn't said much while we worked. Just done as asked and silently communicated with his facial expressions every time our eyes met.

"I'm doing as well as can be when I'm freaking out." It's already hot as hell in the studio from all of us working together, despite the industrial AC Natalie has running. Sweat feels like it's pouring down my back and between my breasts, and my stomach is a ball of knots. I even skipped lunch when Grayson and Winston left to pick up subs from Pickle & Rye because I was worried about nervous nausea.

"Why don't we head out and change into our outfits for tonight? It'll give you time to relax." He grabs my hand and guides us to the exit. "Don't worry about leaving either because everything is pretty much done. Right, Natalie?"

"Right." She shoos us away before sinking into a chair. "Get out of here. We won't be too far behind you."

Grateful for the reprieve, I focus on steadying my nerves while Grayson takes the lead. Driving me home. Making tea in the Keurig while I switch into black leggings, a hot pink tee, and matching leg warmers and scrunchie to match the 80s vibe. He's being so sweet I almost cry from the heightened emotions charging through my veins.

But I rein it in.

At least until we arrive back at the Reaper's Wolves MC compound. Grayson leaves me in the truck while he changes clothes and fetches Tiny—understanding my need for privacy rather than being surrounded by a group of club members—and the tears choose that moment to well up. I dreamed about a man who'd care for me during these episodes. Dreamed of the day I wouldn't be alone to handle them.

But I never expected a bearded biker to fill the role.

To be honest, I figured it would always remain a dream, a fantasy.

Just goes to show that I should expect more for myself. Romantically. Professionally. And once again, I'm thankful for the push Grayson and Natalie gave me to pursue this dance studio idea.

It could fail, but what if it doesn't?

And what if this relationship with Grayson doesn't either?

CHAPTER FIFTEEN

GRAYSON

Everyone shows up to support my girl tonight.

Caroline, Snow. Faith, Alaska. Then the rest of the book club women: Lindy, Kat, and Beth. They are all here for Amelie to watch her succeed, and I couldn't be fucking prouder. Despite her earlier worries, Amelie is a natural with people.

She welcomes each newcomer with warmth and genuine interest. Teaches a couple of easy moves for guests to use throughout the evening.

The sign-up sheet laid out on the entry table by the door is filled—front and back—with students of all ages interested in taking a class led by Amelie.

I've stuck by her side while she met a ton of men and women excited to explore an inclusive dance class that will be judgment-free. My little goddess isn't the only one who has a story of bullying and unsupportive teachers.

I'm just glad she's changing her story and offering the same chance to others.

Some of the dancers from Club Wolf also stop by, along with Georgia. I introduce Luxe and Starr to everyone and Snow gets a weird look on his face before it passes when Starr gives a small wave.

Wonder what his deal is with her? Deciding to ask him about it later, I push it to the back of my mind.

Tonight is about Amelie. Not Snow and whatever issue he has with a woman he's never met before.

"How are you holding up?" I ask Amelie as the evening draws to a close. Party-goers are starting to trickle out the door while Natalie and Caroline begin clean-up.

"Better than expected. Everyone was so *nice*," she stresses the word like it's unfathomable people would accept her. *Oh, my sweet girl.* Amelie naturally puts people at ease. I noticed it at the club with the other dancers who flocked to her. And it happened again tonight.

People feel welcome around her. Relaxed.

"Doesn't surprise me, babe. You've got to believe in yourself more."

"Trust me, I'm working on it." She offers a soft smile before lifting on her toes to press an innocent kiss to my lips. "You're a big part of that, too. Encouraging me. Treating my success like it's a foregone conclusion."

"Because to me, it is." There is no doubt in my mind that whatever Amelie puts her mind to, whether it's teaching dance classes or something else, she will flourish.

And even when a roadblock inevitably crops up, I'll still be here supporting her, helping her through it. Because I'm in this for the long haul.

Forever.

CHAPTER SIXTEEN

AMELIE

Grayson drives me home and agrees to spend the night when I hesitantly ask him to. After spending last night and all day with me, a part of me worries he might need a break, but I should've known better. We fall into bed together, and I revel in his protective embrace as exhaustion finally gets the best of me.

Today was a good day.

Maybe I can do this entrepreneur thing after all.

THE NEXT MORNING WHEN I wake up, Grayson's tattooed skin is too much to resist, so I give in and dot playful kisses across his chest and shoulders, enjoying the fact that he's here in my bed. His arms wrap around me and roll us over, but I stop him from going further with a palm to his chest. "I need to shower. I was too tired last night."

"No problem." He scoops me up like I'm a featherweight instead of a heavyweight and treks toward the bathroom. Carefully, Grayson sets me down and fiddles with the shower knob, waiting for it to warm up before letting me inside and squeezing a large dollop of body wash into his hand.

"Lean your head back, baby. Let me take care of you." He lathers my entire body with gentle circular motions, and everywhere he touches tingles with sparked arousal. I should probably feel self-conscious about Grayson exploring every hill and valley of my body, but whether it's leftover excitement from last night or me finally settling into a new confidence, all I feel is warm contentment.

Not an anxious thought or nervous knot to be found.

And when it's my turn to return the favor, I don't waste time worrying about being awkward since I've never showered with a man before. Grayson doesn't care, so why should I?

All that matters is the here and now.

And here, now, and all his muscles feel pretty damn good.

Once we're clean from head to toe, Grayson backs me into the wet tile and lifts one of my legs to wrap around his waist. *Hmm, I was wondering if we'd be leaving this shower without an orgasm to spare.*

"Hang on, gorgeous."

I do as he says, clenching his arms tight as his cock easily slides between my folds and into my soaking pussy.

What a way to start the morning.

I could get used to morning sex. Oral in bed. Fucked in the shower. It's all amazing.

"God, how is it possible for you to feel this good? I swear your pussy was made for me."

"Maybe it was," I tease, arching into Grayson's thrusts. His palms slap the tile above my shoulders as he grunts with each harsh plunge of his cock. My body shakes from the momentum, not to mention the fiery need coiling in my core.

This isn't the lazy climb of earlier. This is a hasty race to the finish line as both of us groan in relief when the pleasure crests into unrelenting waves.

Eventually, the water turns cold while we struggle to catch our breaths, and my phone can be heard ringing from the bedroom. Ignoring it, I return to licking up the droplets of water sliding over Grayson's pecs, but the ringing starts up again with another call.

"Crap!" I bundle up in a towel before hurrying out of the steamy bathroom to grab the phone in case it's important. Caroline's name appears on the screen.

"Hey, what's up?"

"Natalie and I got to talking last night and we agreed that a celebration is in order."

"For what?" I ask, running through the list of possible birthdays or anniversaries I could've missed. What's so vital that she couldn't give me a morning of freedom with Grayson?

Not that she knows Grayson is here, but still.

"For you!" Caroline exclaims as hushed murmurs sound in the background. She must be at the clubhouse rather than the private cabin she and Snow live in. "For having a successful launch party. So, we decided we're taking you out for girls' night at Club Wolf this evening. It's Sunday, which according to Georgia is a slower business day for them, meaning we won't be so crushed."

"But I have work tomorrow. We all do." There's a reason Sundays are slow. No one wants to party the night before they're expected to wake up at 6 a.m. for work.

Ride this high. Let yourself be celebrated.

This morning I woke up energized with optimism. Am I going to stop the good times and revert to my overly cautious self? The one who doesn't have wild adventures?

Hell no.

"Nevermind. Count me in."

CHAPTER SEVENTEEN

GRAYSON

"To Amelie!" Kat shouts above the thundering music. Everyone raises their shot of tequila and then swallows it in quick succession as Snow, Alaska, Timber, and I sit a couple of tables away, keeping an eye on our women. I'm all for celebrating Amelie's recent accomplishments, but I also know the kinds of men who hang out at Club Wolf. No way I'm letting my girl party without me around to ensure she's safe.

"What's your deal with Starr?" I ask Snow, satisfied for the moment that everything's good with Amelie. For some reason, I can't shake the weird reaction he had to her last night.

"I thought she looked familiar."

"I just hired her. Have you been in the club recently?"

He shakes his head, then Timber pitches in, "Who does she look like to you because there's a niggling sense that I recognize her, too."

Snow takes a drink as his eyes narrow. "Tiffany."

His answer surprises me. "Tiffany the biker bunny you kicked out last year?"

"One in the same."

"Could they be related?"

"Hell if I know. It's not like Tiffany and I exchanged personal info. We fucked, that's it. Even if she wanted more."

And she wanted more. I remember hearing about an angry and naked Tiffany leaving the compound after being kicked out of Snow's private cabin. The guys had a good laugh that night over our club president's woman troubles.

"Do you remember Tiffany's last name?" Ollie pipes up from across the table, his phone already in his hands to tap something out.

"Robinson, I think."

As Ollie works his technological magic, there's an explosive bang at the back of the club and someone shouts "Fire!"

An eerie orange light dances across the main stage where the current dancer skips her finale to jump to safety.

"What the hell?"

All of the guys immediately move to protect the women as flames lick at the stage curtains before rapidly jumping to a table up front, causing the men there to scurry away.

Chaos unfolds as everyone runs for the exit.

"We've gotta get out of here," Snow orders. He tucks his wife under his arm as Alaska does the same with Faith.

I'm about to grab Amelie when she puts a hand on my chest. "I'm fine. I'll go with Lindy and Timber. You should find Georgia."

Shit. My sister. My gaze whips around to the bar where I see Ranger dragging Georgia down the hall to the private exit. That's one person taken care of. But what about the dancers? A large beam falls on the stage blocking any path backstage to the dressing rooms, and my decision is taken away from me.

"Georgia will be safe with Ranger, but we need to leave before another beam falls and hits us."

I urge Amelie's head down and against my chest as I cover her with my arm, barreling through the crowd of people exiting the club. The floor is a mess of broken glasses and splintered chairs from the stampede of scared customers, and a fleeting thought towards the cost of replacing everything springs to mind.

Smoke clouds the air. Visibility drops with each passing second until we finally escape outside where the blare of a fire truck screams in the air. A few minutes later it arrives along with a trail of police cars.

Lindy gasps at the sight of one officer, and Timber wraps an arm around her shoulders. Fuck, her abusive ex, Dean, is one of the cops on the scene.

When it rains, it fucking pours.

"It'll be okay. He'll never hurt you again," Timber promises, glaring at Dean over Lindy's head. Thankfully, the cop is smarter than he looks and doesn't approach them, though he does stare.

Hopefully, he remembers the file of misdeeds we have on him and his friends. A file we won't hesitate to put in the right hands if he chooses to mess with Lindy. Or screw us over while dealing with the fire.

I send Amelie back to the compound with the rest of the women, Snow and Timber, their escorts, while Alaska stays with me to deal with the clusterfuck this evening has turned into.

Hours pass slowly as the fire crew works tirelessly to put out the flames engulfing the building. Once the fire reached our alcohol store though, it was all over. The whole club didn't stand a chance of salvaging with the way the blaze disintegrated everything in its path.

"Any idea what happened?" An officer approaches us—someone other than Dean, thank fuck.

"We've been dealing with a string of accidents lately. Those may be connected to this. An escalation." And what an escalation. The perpetrator went from screwing with dancers' costumes to cutting our power to fucking setting the whole club ablaze.

"We might have a lead on a suspect." Ollie joins our group. "One of the dancers, Starr, was recently hired. Her real name is Candace Blackstone, and she's related to a woman who might have a vendetta against our club, Tiffany Robinson. They're half-sisters which explains the different last names or else we might have made the connection before."

Seriously?

Georgia and I vet our people just like I told Amelie, but apparently, I didn't dig deep enough if I missed this connection. Amelie could've been hurt tonight. All it would've taken was that fallen beam to land a few feet closer. Or she could've been backstage showing her friends the behind-the-scenes of her dancing persona.

The officer nods and scribbles in his notepad.

"Good work, Ollie," I say, wondering if Starr really is the one behind everything. I don't know the woman well, but if she's related to crazy Tiffany, then anything is possible.

Scrubbing a hand over my beard, a weary sigh escapes. Tonight was supposed to be about celebrating Amelie, instead everything blew up in our faces. The one evening when all of us decided to hang out at Club Wolf.

"I don't think it's a coincidence this happened while we were here," I say, sharing my suspicions that this was specifically planned for us.

"Even though this came together last minute?"

"Maybe it was too good of an opportunity to pass up—taking out all of us at once. Or at least having us witness this massive amount of destruction up close and personal." I don't know if the one responsible is Starr, but whoever it is, they have a real vendetta against the Reaper's Wolves.

Is it too much to ask for people to leave us the fuck alone?

Based on the past year? Apparently.

CHAPTER EIGHTEEN

AMELIE

"Do you think they'll rebuild the club?" Beth asks from her curled position on the sofa.

Caroline shrugs and sips from the hot tea she made all of us when we arrived at the clubhouse. Snow decided we should all wait here rather than their private cabin, so his men would have easier access for keeping him abreast of what's happening at Club Wolf.

Grayson and Alaska arrived moments ago after staying at the club all night. Everyone is exhausted but too wired to sleep, hoping the information Ollie gave the police will finally put an end to all these accidents. However, a part of me still doubts that Starr is the one behind everything.

Why would she sabotage her own workplace? It doesn't make sense.

"If I have any say in it, we're rebuilding," Georgia says. All night she's alternated between silence and angry venting, pissed at whatever occurred to set the fire off in the first place.

"And hiring a security team." Caroline sighs, glancing over at the men talking at the cleared poker table. "Logan doesn't want to because all the Reaper's Wolves members are well-equipped to protect themselves and their property, but they joined the MC for a peaceful brotherhood. To leave that kind of life behind. There's a local security company in Suitor's Crossing I'm going to contact. Austin uses them for the Ole Aces security, and if it's good enough for Logan's best friend, then it's good enough for him."

I quietly agree. These guys are pulling double duty running their club businesses while also maintaining extra security. Having a dedicated team outside of the club would be perfect.

A phone rings and the men's chatter dies down as Snow answers. After a couple of questions, he hangs up and waves everyone to the center of the clubhouse living room. "That was the Everton sheriff. They arrested Starr. Tiffany moved in with her after leaving the club. Looks like she stole Starr's live-in boyfriend and her savings before the couple took off. Guess Starr's been stewing for months and finally decided to take her anger out on someone. Since Tiffany is nowhere to be found, she decided Club Wolf was the next best option. Sabotaging our business and cutting into our livelihoods."

"Damn." Kat whistles and everyone else shares the same expression of shock.

"They found Starr trying to dispose of the gas can she used to douse the back hall with gasoline before lighting it on fire. It didn't take much for her to break down and admit to everything. Screwing with the dancers' outfits. Poisoning the staff coffee pot which resulted in the short-staffed night we had. The power outage and now the fire. She'll be going to jail for a long fucking time."

"Wow..." I never had a problem with Starr, and I never would've pegged her as a criminal, but I guess we never know what's going on in people's personal lives.

You never really know when your life can change. Be upended. Which is why you've got to live life to the fullest while you can.

Suddenly, a decision crystallizes in my mind as I type out an email and press send. Things could've gone badly last night with the fire. We're all lucky we got out safely. But the night could've ended differently.

"How are you feeling?" Grayson asks as he hugs me to his chest.

"Good. Surprisingly not anxious, even though I just sent in my two weeks' notice."

"Seriously? Are you sure? I'm not doubting you'll be successful, but emotions are running high right now. I don't want you to regret this decision once things calm down."

Sweet, sweet man.

"Trust me. I'm calm. This is what I want. I'm all in with the dance studio." I bite my lip, then bite the bullet. "And I'm all in with you."

A huge smile beams through Grayson's beard. "Happy to hear it, babe, because I've been all in from the moment you sat next to me at the vet's office. So has Tiny." He winks.

"Mabel is going to have a field day with her new doggy brother." I joke, but my laugh is swiftly stolen by Grayson's mouth swooping down and kissing the hell out of me. A round of hooting and hollering rises around us, but I ignore them.

This moment is all about me and my man.

Looks like I had it in me to snag a hot biker for myself all along.

Me, Amelie Swanson, no need for another—*sexier, more exciting*—persona, after all.

EPILOGUE

GRAYSON

"Five, six, seven, eight!" Amelie calls out to her class of ten-year-olds. Her dance studio was an overnight success. So much so, that it became obvious that more than one instructor was necessary. Which is when my little goddess stole Luxe from Club Wolf to teach with her instead.

Not that I mind.

I love seeing my girl live her dream and reaping mounds of success.

The past few months have been a whirlwind between cementing Amelie's business in Suitor's Crossing and rebuilding Club Wolf in Everton. And moving out of the clubhouse to our own place, an exposed brick loft that just so happened to become available above the dance studio space.

Damn, my life is fucking perfect.

Tiny barks, immediately distracting the kids from their dance routine as they skip over to give him all the pets. He's the studio's unofficial mascot while Mabel spends her days lazing in the front window, looking out at Main Street and soaking in the sun. The two of them aren't best friends or anything, but they tolerate each other which is good enough for me.

"Hey, babe, I brought you a coffee from Brewed." I present the iced caramel macchiato with a flourish and Amelie snatches the shot of caffeine like it's a lifeline.

"Thank you! Guess that means I should forgive you for interrupting class." She grins before tilting her head back for a kiss. It amazes me how open she's become. How far away from that shy woman she used to be.

Don't get me wrong, she still has her moments, but Amelie has stepped fully into her confidence and I love it. Being part of her life, being the one she shares her vulnerabilities with, is a privilege I don't take for granted.

"You should," I agreed before reclaiming her lips for a longer kiss. A chorus of giggles suddenly surround us, and Amelie playfully slaps my chest, pushing me away.

"Ms. Amelie, are you and Mr. Grim in love?" asks a little girl with a huge bow in her hair. Her friends clap in eager anticipation and stare up at us with hearts in their eyes. They're fucking adorable, and I can't wait until Amelie has our own daughter who will take after her mama.

"Yes, we are." Amelie's bright smile wraps around my heart and squeezes tight. "We are very much in love, aren't we, Mr. Grim?"

"Damn right, little goddess."

Always and forever.

CHAPTER ONE

LINDY

You'll always be mine.

That's all the folded white card says. The printed cursive swirls across the otherwise blank space, and I flip the card over searching for any other clues as to who it's from. A vase of yellow daisies sat on the welcome mat of my porch this morning. I almost tipped them over in my rush to get out the door and to my standing coffee date with Caroline at Brewed.

Sure, we could chat and drink coffee here at the Reaper's Wolves MC compound, but where's the fun in that? It's nice to hang out in the cute downtown of Suitor's Crossing and enjoy a casual friend date—something I'm still getting used to after a year of living isolated with my abusive ex.

Don't think about Dean.

But it's difficult when I read those four words again: *You'll always be mine.* Would Dean be stupid enough to threaten me after all this time? And on a freaking biker compound? Especially when I know the club has dirt on him. Dirt they won't hesitate to release if he decides to fuck with my life again.

But who else would send me flowers and a card?

My friends would snicker and point out the obvious, at least to them. *Timber.* My crazy hot shadow. A tall, bearded military veteran who's appointed himself as my personal protector. But this doesn't seem like his style.

Timber may not say much, but a mysterious gift and note don't strike me as the way he'd declare his interest. Like the rest of the men of the MC, when he wants something or someone, I bet he won't hesitate to claim it. In person. Staring you down with those dark eyes of his.

Groaning, I toss the card aside and grab my purse. I'm already going to be late to meet Caroline. I don't need to stand here fantasizing about Timber's captivating gaze. Or what I'd do if he ever actually decided he wants more than being my security guard.

My track record with men sucks.

And my last boyfriend blew all the other jerks out of the water. Because Dean was an abusive asshole. Physically and mentally. It took all of my strength to leave him, and even then, Caroline had to help me.

Timber is nothing like Dean, but can I risk my heart and well-being again?

No fucking way.

Because I don't think I can survive pain like that a second time around.

Don't miss Lindy and Timber's story in *Timber's Girl*[1]!

THANKS FOR READING & DON'T FORGET TO RATE/ REVIEW!

Please consider leaving a rating/review. Ratings & reviews are the #1 way to support an indie author like me.
Also, don't miss out on free books and up-to-date release information. You can sign up for my newsletter here[1].
I appreciate your support!
XO, Hallie

---

1. https://www.thearrowedheart.com/hallie-bennett

ABOUT THE AUTHOR

Hallie prefers steamy, insta-love stories where curvy girls are claimed by filthy-talking heroes. And when she ran out of reading material, she decided to write her own stories. If you want a quick, hot read, she's your girl!

Printed in Great Britain
by Amazon